TANC unfolded its wings and fired up its nuclear-powered turbines, and Tom and his group were away. "Take us back to Swift Enterprises," Tom commanded PIPP, the machine's artificial intelligence brain.

Sandra looked at the radar screen. "We've got trouble," she said. "Surface-to-air missiles, heading straight at us!"

The missiles came closer, plumes of white smoke trailing behind them. "Impact in twenty seconds," PIPP said. "They're locked on and tracking."

"And I know *what* they're tracking!" Tom exclaimed. He stripped off his belt, with the buckle containing the personnel locator. Then he tossed the belt in a small compartment labeled Sample Ejection Port and pressed the Cycle button.

A couple of seconds later, a brilliant flash lit up the TANC's monitors.

"One of the missiles got your belt buckle," said Sandra. "But the others must be heat seekers. They're still following us." Tom saw her swallow hard. "Impact in five seconds."

Books in the Tom Swift® Series

Available from ARCHWAY Paperbacks

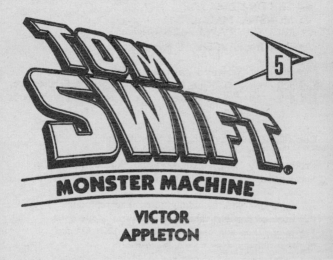

TOM SWIFT

5

MONSTER MACHINE

VICTOR APPLETON

AN ARCHWAY PAPERBACK
Published by POCKET BOOKS
New York   London   Toronto   Sydney   Tokyo   Singapore

AN ARCHWAY PAPERBACK *Original*

An Archway Paperback published by
POCKET BOOKS, a division of Simon & Schuster Inc.
1230 Avenue of the Americas, New York, NY 10020

Copyright © 1991 by Simon & Schuster Inc.

Produced by Byron Preiss Visual Publications, Inc.
Special thanks to James D. Macdonald and Debra Doyle

ISBN: 0-671-67827-2

First Archway Paperback printing October 1991

10 9 8 7 6 5 4 3 2 1

TOM SWIFT, AN ARCHWAY PAPERBACK and colophon
are registered trademarks of Simon & Schuster Inc.

Cover art by Carla Sormanti

Printed in the U.S.A.

IL 6+

WHOO-WHEE!" EXCLAIMED RICK CANTWELL. "What on earth is that?"

The door of the Swift Enterprises robotic hangar slid closed behind Rick and his companion, Mandy Coster. The two teenagers were staring at a huge, four-wheeled vehicle in the center of the workroom floor. The vehicle's body, painted a bright candy-apple red with the Swift Enterprises logo on the side, looked like an outsize pickup truck with a camper on top of the bed. From the bottoms of the tires to the top of the roof, the machine loomed almost twice as tall as its blue-eyed, blond-haired creator, Tom Swift.

Tom himself stood beside a workbench near one wall of the big, echoing hangar—only a

1

small portion of the Swift Enterprises laboratory and workshop complex. Pneumatic lifts and other equipment for working on heavy vehicles filled the hangar's available floor space. Pegboards crammed with tools lined the walls of the hangar, and the workbench was littered with more tools, stray bits of wire, microchips, and scraps of electronic circuit boards.

In response to Rick's question, Tom grinned and gestured at the vehicle. "This? NASA opened up the bidding recently on a great new contract. When Dad saw I was interested, he told me to go ahead and put together a working prototype."

"The National Aeronautics and Space Administration?" Rick inquired. "I can't see it. Big as that thing is, it's way too small to be a spaceship."

Tom's younger sister, Sandra, looked up from where she was punching letters and numbers into a computer keyboard beside the workbench. Cables led from the computer to an insulated box on the side of the bench. "Don't let that four-wheeled gizmo's looks deceive you," she said. "It really works. What you're looking at right now is the Swift Enterprises Transformable, Ambulatory, Nuclearpowered Craft—TANC."

Rick shook his head. "I don't know, Tom,"

2

he said with mock seriousness. "I don't believe NASA goes in much for monster trucks."

Tom laughed. "Just because you have monster trucks on the brain, Rick, doesn't mean everybody does."

The young inventor had to admit, though, that the TANC's brightly painted cab gave it a superficial resemblance to the huge custom-modified pickup trucks he had seen performing spectacular feats on television. The oversize wheels—like tractor wheels but even bigger—that lifted the bottom of the cab an easy five feet off the ground only added to the monster-truck appearance.

"Anyway," Tom added, "the TANC only looks like this when it's in terrestrial mode."

"Wait a minute," said Rick. "A minute ago Sandra called this thing transformable, and now you're talking about terrestrial mode. You mean it changes shape?"

"You got it," Tom said. "By the way, Rick, what brings you to the lab today?" He looked over at Mandy and added hastily, "Not that I don't enjoy your company, but I thought you guys had plans for this afternoon."

"Sure do," said Rick. "We're here to pick up Sandra. She's going over to the Arroyo Seco Autodrome with us."

Tom's sister nodded. "That's right. We're planning to watch some *real* monster trucks in action."

"Now I remember," Tom said to Sandra. "The big rally. I'd forgotten all about it when I asked you to help me finish up in here. Luckily, we're almost done. Rick, can you wait just a few more minutes—"

"Anything I can do to help?"

"Now that you mention it," Tom said, "there is. It's time to test the wings."

"Wings?" Mandy Coster asked. "Why does a truck need wings?"

Tom glanced at Mandy again. The two of them had dated several times, though the relationship wasn't yet serious. She looked as if she really was interested in the vehicle, not just asking about it to flatter Tom.

He cleared his throat. "As you know, NASA is getting ready for our next step into space— an orbiting station, permanent bases on the Moon, and an expedition to Mars. As part of the process, they've opened up the bidding on the next generation of multipurpose exploration vehicles. Swift Enterprises is submitting TANC."

"Wow," said Mandy. "You mean a rocket is going to carry that thing to Mars?"

"Even better," said Tom. "This thing *is* the rocket. It changes shape to meet the needs of the mission."

"Like the Rover?" asked Rick, referring to Swift Enterprises' transformable combination of jet and armored car.

4

"The Rover's transformations are slow," Tom said. "Too slow for what I want this baby to do. Here, help me get these high-speed cameras into place." He pushed one boom-mounted camera around until it pointed at the side of the huge red vehicle.

"This vehicle represents the next generation of Rover technology," Tom said as he helped Rick move a second camera to point at TANC's other side. "It can change shape and function under local, remote, or automatic control. And where the Rover took several minutes to alter shape, TANC can make changes in under a minute. Okay, now we're ready for the test. The wings should deploy too fast for us to see, so we have a slow-motion tape set up."

Tom turned to face a monitor mounted on the wall above his workbench. He touched a switch and red On the Air lights glowed from the fronts of the two cameras he and Rick had just put into place.

"Rick, could you move the left-hand remote down a little?" Tom said, checking the screen. "Ah, that's good."

"Now what?" Rick asked after he'd finished adjusting the camera to point straight at the side of the truck.

Tom picked up a remote-control box from the clutter on his test bench and pushed a button. The twin doors of TANC's cab swung upward like a bird's wings spreading.

"Go up into TANC and press the third button from the top on the control panel," Tom said. "You can't miss it—it's labeled Paul McCartney."

"Paul McCartney?"

"Yeah. *Wings*."

Rick groaned.

Tom turned his concentration to the monitor screen as Rick climbed the short chrome ladder to the cockpit of the unusual craft. "Ready," he called out. "Get set, go!"

With a high-pitched whir and a blur of motion, TANC sprouted a pair of stubby triangular wings. At almost the same moment an angry voice boomed out from the far side of the big red vehicle.

"Look out, you young fool! You almost took my head off!"

A second later the owner of the voice came into view. He was a distinguished-looking man in late middle age, with close-cropped silver gray hair and rather hard blue eyes. His well-tailored suit had a Swift Enterprises visitor badge hanging from one lapel. Tom's father, Thomas Swift, Sr., followed close behind him.

"Why don't you watch what you're doing?" the man demanded as he came forward. "Somebody could get killed."

"I'm sorry, sir," Tom said, "but the Experiment in Progress sign *was* turned on outside the door. Besides," he added, "TANC has built-in collision-avoidance mechanisms. The wings wouldn't have deployed if you'd actually been in the way."

"It's all right, Tom," Mr. Swift cut in. "Mr. Bradshaw and I came here to pick up the Tallis Particle Generator for a demonstration. Have you finished the low-power modifications on it yet?"

"All done, Dad," said Tom. "I took it over to the main workshop this morning."

"Excellent," said Tom's father. "We're going there next. Meanwhile, please continue working on TANC."

Mr. Swift departed, accompanied by the still-frowning Bradshaw. As the door closed after them, Rick shook his head. "You know, Tom, I don't think that guy likes you."

"Who was he, anyway?" asked Mandy.

"That was Arthur Bradshaw," said Tom. "President of the Bradshaw Group—they're an import-export firm specializing in high-tech goods. He's trying to strike some kind of deal with Swift Enterprises, buying Swift products for resale and saving us the hassle of having to deal with the red tape."

"I don't think Dad likes him, though," said Sandra. "He called Bradshaw a schemer and a war profiteer the other day while he was reading the newspaper during breakfast."

"Oh, *that* Bradshaw!" exclaimed Mandy. "He's in the papers all the time. Your dad's pretty close to right about him, too—he uses loopholes in the law to get away with selling weapons to terrorists and revolutionaries."

"Don't worry," said Tom. "He's not likely to get anything out of Swift Enterprises. But I need to get back to work. Now that we've run the manual tests, it's time to install TANC's *real* boss."

He opened a refrigerated box next to his workbench. Heavy vapor began to drift out and downward.

"We're using an experimental form of super-conducting circuits here," Tom announced. "This is the important part of the machine. I've invented a Polymorphic Integrated Parallel Processor—a PIPP—to act as TANC's brain. Most computers and robots don't actually think—they only reflect their programming. But TANC has the ability to learn, to make real decisions, to make guesses and act on them.

"So far," Tom continued, "the PIPP has had a whole library of information stored in it, but it hasn't had any real-life experience. It programs itself, though, just like a child learning, and it'll never repeat a mistake."

Using robotic handlers to protect himself

from the cold, Tom lifted the PIPP out of the cold box and walked it carefully over to TANC. He opened an access plate on the side of the vehicle's cab. More cold vapor puffed out.

Tom eased the PIPP into the opening. Magnetic couplers grabbed it with a soft click, locking it into place. Then Tom closed the access plate. The skin of the vehicle slid in place over the opening so that no clue to the PIPP's location remained.

"There," he said. He checked his watch. "Rick, if you guys plan to make the truck rally in Arroyo Seco, you'd better leave right now."

Without warning, before any of the others could answer, a horn began bleating over the lab's speaker systems.

"Security alert, security alert!" blared an amplified voice, making the big, high-ceilinged room vibrate with multiple echoes. "Class Three security alert!"

SECURITY ALERT!" THE SPEAKER SYSTEM blared again. "Attempted break-in at Warehouse Nine!"

Tom looked worried. "That's the third break-in this week," he said. He raised his voice for the hangar's sound pickups. "Harlan, can you give us an update?"

A holographic image of Harlan Ames, Swift Enterprises' head of security, appeared in the robotic hangar. The lean, silver-haired man had a disgusted look on his face. "We didn't catch them this time, either, Tom. We have parts missing, and a big hole in the south face of the warehouse. The security camera on that side was disabled, and the guard in that block was injured. I'll have to wait for the docs to clear him before I can ask any questions. Nothing more we can do now. The base will be shut until my personnel have time to clear the grounds."

"Any problem with me taking TANC out to the proving ground?" Tom asked.

"No, you should be okay there," Harlan replied. "Keep your eyes open." The image winked out.

Mandy shook her head. "If the gates at Swift Enterprises are shut until Harlan is finished with his investigation, there's no way we'll be able to make it to the Arroyo Seco Autodrome."

She looks really disappointed, Tom thought. "It may not be quite as exciting," he offered, "but I'll be testing TANC in a few minutes. You people want to come along?"

Mandy smiled. "Sure thing!"

"Let's go, then," said Tom, and the four teenagers climbed aboard the big vehicle.

TANC's interior was roomier than it looked from the outside. Up front, behind a thick windshield, two high-backed, padded seats faced a dashboard filled with an impressive array of screens and readouts. Instead of a rear wall behind the seats, a passageway opened up to the rear of the cab—the part that, seen from the outside, looked like a camper shell. In the back portion of the vehicle four more padded seats faced toward the front on pedestal mounts. More monitor screens and instrument panels lined TANC's inside walls.

Tom and the others sat down and fastened their seatbelts. Actually, the safety restraints were a system of harnesses and webbing that would have looked more at home in a jet fighter than in a pickup truck.

"How do you drive this thing?" Rick asked. "I don't see any steering wheel."

"Don't worry," Tom replied. "The AI—artificial intelligence—I just installed takes care of all that. Watch." The young inventor crossed his arms over his chest. "PIPP, close the doors and retract wings."

The two side doors of TANC folded down and locked with a click, and the wings vanished into the sides of the machine. "Thanks, PIPP," said Tom. "Now take us outside."

Smoothly and gently the huge vehicle came to life. The sound of its engine was a faint hum, little more than a vibration in the carpeted floor underfoot. TANC pivoted until it was pointed directly at the locked door of the garage. Then it started crawling forward.

Already Rick was looking impressed. "How does TANC turn in such a small radius?"

"Each of the wheels is independently powered," Tom replied. "With the two right wheels going forward and the two left wheels going in reverse, TANC can turn in place. And that's just one of TANC's— Whoa! PIPP, stop!"

TANC came to an instant halt—a fraction of an inch from the still-closed door of the garage.

"Oops," said Tom. "I didn't say to *open* the door."

"Sorry," came another voice in the cab, one that belonged neither to Rick nor to the girls. "I didn't know it was required. This vehicle is capable of driving through a closed door."

"It's okay, PIPP," Tom said. "We're all learning here. Actually," he added in an aside to his friends, "PIPP was understating things quite a bit. TANC has enough power to smash right through a cinder-block wall."

"That was the truck talking?" asked Mandy.

"More or less," Tom said. "It's part of the AI brain's verbal interface. On a mission in space PIPP will function as another member of the crew."

"Pleased to meet you," said the voice. "Allow me to introduce myself. My name is PIPP."

"PIPP," said Tom, "I'd like you to meet my friends Rick and Mandy and my sister, Sandra. Please take voiceprints of them. You can take orders from them as well as from me, but from no one else unless I direct it."

Tom turned to his friends. "Could you say something one at a time to introduce yourselves?"

"Richard Cantwell," said Rick. "Pleased to meet you."

"The pleasure is mine," PIPP replied.

"Hi! I'm Mandy," Mandy said.

"Charmed."

"And you know me," said Sandra. "My brother had me feeding you data files for the last three weeks."

"Ah, yes ... Sandra Swift. Thank you for filling me in with those last bits of information."

"Okay, PIPP," Tom said. "Everyone's been introduced. You can go ahead and unlock the garage doors."

"Right," said PIPP. A light on TANC's control panel blinked briefly, and the garage doors slid open.

"Great," Tom said. "Now take us to the Swift Enterprises proving ground."

TANC started forward again. Turning right at the edge of the airfield, the robot vehicle made its way east across the Swift Enterprises complex, turning at all the proper cross streets, halting at pedestrian crosswalks, and going down the road as smoothly and accurately as if it were running on tracks.

In the front right-hand seat Rick Cantwell looked dissatisfied. "This thing is going to take all the fun out of driving," he complained.

"Don't worry," Tom reassured his friend.

"The real fun has only just started. The beauty of using artificial intelligence is that it leaves the human pilot free to work on important stuff, instead of concentrating on the road."

As they spoke, TANC rolled past the large administration building. More cars than usual filled the visitor parking spaces out front. One of the visitors' cars was a silver-and-black stretch limousine, with the Bradshaw Group's stylized BG logo on the door.

TANC passed the administration building and then went by the day care center for the children of Swift employees. From there the experimental vehicle went on past the automated factories and at last approached the high fence of the Swift Enterprises complex.

TANC glided to a stop at the gate that led to the rugged hills of the proving grounds. Today the gate was closed and the guard shack occupied. The guard—a member of Harlan Ames's highly trained internal security team—stepped forward. She waved TANC to a halt.

"Good afternoon," the guard called. "Who's there and where are you going?"

"Open my door, PIPP," Tom said.

The winglike door on TANC's left side hinged up. Tom smiled down at the guard.

"Good afternoon, Jenny," he said. "How's the search coming?"

The guard's eyes widened in recognition. "Oh, it's you, Tom," she said. "You haven't heard? Some items are still missing. But I don't suppose I need to check you."

Tom held up a hand. "No, no. That's all right," he said. "If Harlan thinks all vehicles ought to be checked, I'll back him up. Look anywhere you want."

The guard climbed up the chrome ladder to the cab and glanced into the rear. "No contraband up here," she said. "Could you pop open the cargo compartment?"

"PIPP?" said Tom. A light glowed on TANC's control panel, and a cargo compartment opened in the vehicle's flank. The security guard climbed back down the ladder and looked inside. Then she checked beneath the TANC, using a mirror mounted on a rod to look at the undercarriage. After she'd finished, she stepped back.

"You're clean," the guard said. "The things we're looking for are fairly bulky. One more thing, Tom—no one is to enter map coordinates G-three through H-nineteen while your father is demonstrating the Tallis Particle Generator for Mr. Bradshaw. Oh, and do you mind telling me when you expect to come back through, so I can warn my relief that you're out here?"

"I shouldn't be on the proving ground for more than a couple of hours," Tom replied.

"And I'll be careful to stay away from the generator demonstration. Dad and I developed that thing as part of TANC's eventual basic tool kit for asteroid mining. Even on low power it can slice through concrete like a knife through cheese."

"Okay, thanks," the guard said, stepping back and hitting a control box on her belt. The gate swung open.

"PIPP, close my door, then go through," Tom said.

"Door closed," the AI brain responded as TANC suited its action to the words. "Is there anywhere in particular you'd like to go?"

Tom thought for a minute. "There's a small range of hills just east of here," he said finally, "and I'd like to see what kind of slopes TANC can handle. PIPP, find the nearest ten-percent grade."

During the next half hour Tom—with PIPP doing the driving—took TANC over a series of hills, each one higher and steeper than the last. PIPP handled TANC a bit clumsily at first, but the brain's performance grew better with each minor mistake and subsequent correction.

"So far TANC exceeds design specs," Tom said as they came to the top of a seventy-five–degree slope. "PIPP, you're doing really well."

"Too well, if you ask me," said Rick. "This is about as interesting as watching paint dry.

Too bad you forgot to build in a radio, to while away those long, dull years between planets."

"I didn't forget," Tom said. "I just don't have the entertainment and communications systems on-line yet. We're testing TANC one step at a time, and the quality-of-life luxury touches come last. Right now the only radio in TANC is my personal Swift pocket phone."

Next came the obstacle course, as TANC made its way over, under, and through a series of dirt walls and ditches. The course concluded with a slalom run through ten-foot-tall concrete pylons, set into an asphalt track with just enough space between them for the TANC to pass. Tom marked down the results on his pocket note-recorder.

"Exceeds design specs again," he said. "Only one more thing to try: broken terrain speed trials. PIPP, take me to the northwest corner of the proving ground the fastest way you can."

The vehicle started forward, picking up speed as it went. "How fast can this thing go?" Rick asked as the velocity readout flickered past fifty kilometers per hour.

"The NASA contract calls for forty-five kilometers per hour on land," Tom said as the asphalt underneath the vehicle's huge wheels turned to dirt. TANC was running off-road now, over open ground, but the change made no difference to the smooth ride inside the cab. "What I want to find out is how much more speed we have."

"Tom," said Mandy from one of the pedestal seats in the rear compartment, "about the map on this panel here . . ."

Tom looked around. Mandy was pointing at one of the computer screens arranged along the inside wall of the TANC. The display showed a three-dimensional holographic map of the Swift Enterprises proving grounds. She was pointing to the deep canyon where Swift Enterprises tested such devices as their jet-assisted hang glider. Near the tip of Mandy's finger, a glowing green dot moved across the holographic display, drawing closer by the second to the rim of the canyon.

"Uh-oh," said Sandra, looking over Mandy's shoulder. "That's *us*. And we're getting real near the edge."

Tom snapped his head back around to look outside the front window. Sandra was right. Rocks and underbrush slid past in a brown-and-green blur, and the cliff's edge made a dark line against the overcast sky.

"PIPP, stop!" Tom shouted. "This isn't part of the test!"

TANC shuddered as PIPP slammed on the brakes. But it was too late. The heavy vehicle's momentum took them all the way to the edge of the cliff.

For a split second TANC hung there, poised on the brink of the chasm. The rim crumbled as the vehicle's immense mass tilted forward. Then they fell, hurtling toward the jagged rocks more than six hundred feet below.

3

THE ROBOT VEHICLE PLUMMETED TOWARD THE
bottom of the canyon. Only the seat belts and
safety webbing kept its passengers from being
thrown about the interior of the TANC's cab
as it fell.

"PIPP!" Tom shouted. "Transform to basic
airframe configuration!"

The inside of the vehicle didn't change, but
the forward part of the craft shrank so that it
looked less like the front of a truck and more
like the needle nose of an airplane. Triangular
wings snapped out from TANC's sides, and
servomotors whined as the monster wheels
folded up beneath the cab. The entire process
had taken seconds to complete.

"Flight attitude normal, maximum power!" Tom called out.

TANC's jets fired, filling the cab with their deep-throated roar. Sudden acceleration pushed Tom and his companions backward against the padded seats. TANC was no longer falling—the ground shrank away beneath them as the craft picked up speed and gained altitude. A few moments more and they broke through the low cloud layer to a clear blue sky.

Rick gave an admiring whistle. "Man, that was slick," he said. "So that's what the wings are for."

"This is just one of TANC's standard operating modes," Tom said. "Jet airplane."

Rick shook his head in mock amazement. "Jet airplane, spaceship, monster truck—next you're going to tell me that it's an electric submarine, too."

"No," Tom said, pulling out his electronic notepad. He thumbed the pad on and said, "Take a note: Check feasibility of adding submersible configuration to the TANC's operating modes."

The little notebook burped. Tom's words appeared on the screen, and a printout appeared below. He tore off the slip of paper and tucked it into his pocket before turning back to Rick. "I'll check it out when we get back to the robotic hangar."

"But I was only . . ." Rick sighed. "Never mind."

"Excuse me," Mandy cut in from behind Tom's shoulder, "but where exactly are we headed?"

"Let's take a look," said Tom. He touched a couple of the pressure pads on the front control panel. Two of the screens in back lit up, one with a radar view of the area and another with a high-resolution television picture of the airspace around them.

"Here we are," he said. "Just a little way from— Hey! Wait a minute! Add some left rudder!"

TANC had gone into a sideslip, losing altitude fast as its right wing tilted downward. At Tom's command the craft straightened out and began to climb again.

"I think," said Tom, "that we need a bit of practice before we go anywhere. PIPP, tune in the very-high-frequency beacons at Swift Enterprises and Central Hills Municipal Airport for your cross bearings. Then fly around for a bit to gather data on flight configuration and execution. Don't go below two thousand feet. I'll tell you if you're doing anything wrong."

"Shouldn't we alert the airport that we're low-altitude traffic and give them our location?" Mandy asked.

"Can't," said Tom. "Like I told Rick, we

don't have the communications gear installed in this thing yet. Besides," he added, "FAA regulations don't require a private aircraft even to have a radio."

"What instruments *does* the FAA say we need?" Mandy asked.

"A compass and a clock," Sandra said. "TANC's got them both. We're still over the proving grounds, anyway, so the airspace is restricted to Swift Enterprises traffic."

After half an hour or so of flying, PIPP was handling TANC as well in the air as on the ground. The AI brain finished the experiment with a few basic stunt maneuvers.

"Okay," said Tom. "That's about enough."

"You're not kidding," said Sandra. "I think I left my stomach behind on that last loop."

"Speaking of stomachs," Rick said, "mine's running on empty. Is there any chow on board?"

"Sorry," Tom replied, "but this version of the TANC is only a prototype—it doesn't carry supplies. How do you feel about a burger when we get back home?"

"Sounds great to me."

"Fine," said Tom. "Take us to the airfield, PIPP."

The formerly lumbering but now graceful jet swooped, turned, and went into a gentle dive. "Locked on the beam," PIPP said. "On final."

The jet broke through the low cloud layer and started descending toward the runway below.

"Uh, Tom," Sandra said as the jet coasted to the end of the runway, stopped, and resumed its land-based shape. "This doesn't look like the Swift Enterprises airfield."

Tom glanced out the front window, and then at one of the display screens. "You're right," he said. "It isn't. PIPP, what happened?"

"As you requested, I have taken you to the airfield. This is the Arroyo Seco airstrip," said the AI brain. "Did I do something wrong? I'm sorry."

"It's all right," Tom said. "I just wasn't specific enough when I gave you instructions. We live, we learn."

"What do we do now, Tom?" asked Mandy.

"Now we see how the TANC handles on the open road," Tom said. "PIPP, do you know where we are?"

"Yes," replied the synthesized voice.

"Can you get us back to the Swift Enterprises complex by way of mapped roads, obeying all traffic laws?"

"I can."

"Good," said Tom. "Then let's go."

"What powers TANC?" Mandy asked as the vehicle left the taxiway and headed for the exit from the small airfield. "Looking at it, I wouldn't think it was big enough to carry fuel for what we just did."

"It's nuclear-powered, remember?" Tom replied. "We're using my dad's miniature fusion power modules. I figured out how to get them away from fixed locations by using light-weight compressed molecular shielding."

"Speaking of getting away from fixed locations," said Sandra, "maybe you'd better call back home and tell everyone we'll be a little bit late."

"Good idea. I don't want Mom to get worried." Tom reached into his shirt pocket and pulled out a small plastic object about the size of a large matchbox. He thumbed a switch on the side of the case. There was a crackling noise, followed by a high-pitched whine.

"Swift Enterprises Information Center," said a voice. "May I help you?"

"This is Tom Swift calling," Tom said. "Could you send word to my dad that I had to leave the proving ground with TANC? Right now I'm on state road one-thirteen-A, southbound, just outside Arroyo Seco. I'll let you know our ETA when I have it. We're planning to stop for lunch."

"No problem," came the reply. "I'll pass the word."

"Thanks. Tom Swift out."

Tom returned the personal phone to his shirt pocket. TANC continued to roll along the dusty asphalt road on its high, deeply treaded tires. After a few minutes the two-lane blacktop linked up with a busy four-lane highway.

"Everybody, keep your eyes open for a place to eat," said Tom. "Hamburgers, pizza, fried chicken . . . that sort of thing."

"A cross-check of local telephone directories reveals many such dining establishments in the Arroyo Seco area," PIPP said. "Shall I implement a standard search pattern?"

Before Tom could say yes or no, Rick gave a shout and pointed out of TANC's right-hand window. "Look there!"

Tom followed his friend's gesture. He saw a large parking lot filled with cars and pickups, surrounding an open-air sports arena. A banner out front read Monster Truck Rally Today!

Rick grinned at Mandy and Sandra. "Maybe we can catch the show after all."

"I don't know," said Tom. "I really have to get TANC back to the robotic hangar."

"Just drop us off," Rick said. "A bunch of the guys from school are going to be here—we can get a ride back to your place without any trouble."

"What about your hunger pangs?" asked

Tom. "A moment ago you sounded like a guy who was serious about a shake and fries."

Rick laughed. "Not when there's a chance to see some cars get converted to tin pancakes. I'll find some eats at the show. There'll be hot-dog vendors for sure."

"It's your stomach, not mine," said Tom. "PIPP, go into the parking lot over there and find a place for us. Don't run over any cars on the way."

"Understood, Tom," the machine replied, and began to slow in preparation for its turn.

The parking lot around the arena was packed with autos. TANC cruised slowly first down one lane, then another. At the far end of the lot it turned suddenly right, then around to the side. In a roped-off area behind the arena stood a dozen trucks, their bodies sparkling with chrome and glass, their cabs perched high atop giant tires. TANC paused, steered through an opening in the rope, and eased to a halt beside a truck labeled Stompomatic in letters shaped like lightning bolts.

"What are we doing here?" Sandra asked.

"This appears to be the parking area for TANC-like vehicles," PIPP replied.

Tom sighed and ran a hand through his blond hair. "PIPP, just because you look a lot like these vehicles doesn't mean—"

"Uh-oh, Tom," cut in Sandra. "We've got company."

Tom looked out the window. Approaching TANC was a middle-aged man wearing a dusty straw cowboy hat.

"Open the door, PIPP," Tom said. "Let's see what he wants."

The driver's-side door lifted upward in time for Tom to see the man in the cowboy hat checking his clipboard. "I don't see a Swift Enterprises entry on the list," the man said, "but you're in luck. Baron von Crunch is having trouble with his engine. You can take his slot."

"This isn't really—" Tom began, but Rick cut him off.

"Yes, sir, thank you!" Turning to his friend, Rick said, "Come on, Tom, it'll be fun. I've always wanted to see one of these rallies from up close."

Tom glanced at Mandy and his sister. "What do you think?"

"Go for it," advised Mandy.

Sandra nodded. "Think of it as the ultimate field test."

Still Tom hesitated, but the temptation to put his latest invention through a really grueling trial run was hard to resist. If any part of TANC is going to break down under pressure, he told himself, a contest like this will do it.

"Okay," he said finally. "I'll take the slot."

"Right," said the man in the cowboy hat.

"What name do you want on the score-board?"

"TANC," came PIPP's voice over the outboard speakers.

" 'Tank,' you got it," the man said. "You can pay your registration fee and pick up a schedule in the office over there. But you'd better hurry—the prelims are in fifteen minutes."

I CAN'T BELIEVE WE'RE REALLY DOING THIS," muttered Tom as Rick hurried off to the registration booth. "I'd better go after him and tell him I made a mistake."

Before Tom could move, though, he heard the beeping tone of his personal phone. He pulled the small plastic box from his pocket. "Tom Swift here," he responded automatically as the antenna extended itself.

"Tom, this is HQ." Despite the tiny speaker in the personal phone, his father's voice came through clearly. "When do you expect to be back here at the complex?"

"I've been a little delayed. Home by dark, I guess."

"Problems with TANC?"

"No trouble at all," Tom replied. "But I'm at the monster truck rally in Arroyo Seco."

"Stay where you are," his father advised him. "I'm going to send a man named Peter Newell over there to meet you. Show him anything he wants to see, answer anything he wants to ask, and put TANC through its paces for him, okay?"

"Sure thing, Dad," Tom said. "What's up?"

"Newell's a representative from NASA," Mr. Swift replied. "When he heard you had a prototype vehicle already in the testing stages, he was eager to take a look at it."

"Don't worry," Tom said with more confidence than he actually felt. What had started out as a simple test run over the proving grounds was quickly getting more complicated than it needed to be. "By the way—what happened with Mr. Bradshaw?"

"He did make an offer for the Tallis Particle Generator," said Tom's father. "But he wouldn't agree to take the modified low-power version, so I sent him packing. Frankly, I don't like the kind of press he gets. And the aerospace contract is more important, anyway."

"Got you, Dad," said Tom. "I'll show that NASA rep just how much TANC can do." He signed off and busied himself with checking over TANC's vital systems.

"Tom," Mandy asked, "what would somebody like Bradshaw want with a Tallis Particle Generator anyway?"

"Well, it *is* high-tech mining equipment," admitted Tom. "But the unmodified version was designed for deep-space mining—it's powerful enough to plow through an asteroid. Around the lab we called that version the Tallis Cannon. Maybe Bradshaw got word of the joke and wanted to resell the full-power generator as a *real* cannon."

"That's just the sort of thing he'd do," Mandy said. "Supposedly, he's big on buying things that are legal, then showing his customers how to take them apart and turn them into weapons. The *Wall Street Journal* called him 'the world's number-one supplier of do-it-yourself danger kits.'"

"Not a nice guy," observed Sandra. "I'm surprised Dad didn't throw him off the complex so hard he bounced."

Tom cut her a hard look. "That's no way to do business, Sandra. Of course, if there were any proof that Bradshaw was selling customized weapons, Dad wouldn't have let him in in the first place."

As he spoke, Rick came back from the registration booth with his hands full of papers. "Okay, guys, we're in," he said. "There was an entry fee, but I had enough cash on me to cover it."

Tom gave a faint sigh. "Don't worry about

the fee," he said. "This rally just turned into a Swift Enterprises field demonstration, so I can pay you back out of TANC's lab budget. What's our first event?"

Rick consulted his sheaf of papers. "It says here the first event is the Car Crush," he said. "After that comes the Road Race, and then the Tug of War."

"Sounds like fun," Tom said with a smile. He turned to his sister. "Sandra—could you keep an eye on TANC's radar board? If that NASA rep is coming straight over from Swift Enterprises, he's probably coming by air."

"Scope's clear," Sandra replied after a minute. "No, wait, here comes something. Low and slow."

"Does it look like our visitor?" asked Tom.

"Whoever it is, he's transmitting a Swift Enterprises identifier. Look to the left and you should see him—I have him on the high-res screen back here."

"I have a visual on him," Tom said, raising a pair of thin-film binoculars to his eyes. They were another of his own inventions. No larger than a business envelope, they gathered and magnified light like the finest binoculars. Best of all, Tom could fold them up and fit them into his shirt pocket, right behind his personal phone.

"It's a Swift Enterprises portable helicopter, all right," he announced. "That's our man. I'll go out and meet him. You guys wait here."

Tom climbed down the ladder from TANC's cab and walked over to an open area at the edge of the parking lot. The helicopter, a one-man automated machine, would home in on Tom's Swift Enterprises locator device.

The little helicopter landed, and a man emerged. Tall and thin, he stepped out of the helicopter's tiny cockpit and headed toward Tom. As soon as he had emerged, the helicopter began folding itself up into a compact package with a series of clicks, clanks, and whirs.

The tall man glanced back over his shoulder at the collapsing helicopter and raised an eyebrow briefly. "I must say that you Swifts have your own ways of doing things," he said. Turning back toward Tom, he held out his hand. "Peter Newell."

"Tom Swift," Tom replied. He shook Newell's hand, then walked over and put his hand on the now completely folded portable helicopter. "TANC is right over here."

"How can you possibly do that?" Newell asked as Tom casually picked up the folded helicopter. "I'd think even a folding helicopter would be too heavy to lift."

"We've put a lot of work into it," Tom said. "As early as the 1980s there were fully functional aircraft that weighed under sixty pounds. Mostly the trick is to use thin-film materials inflated with air compressed by the engine where strength is needed. The rotors, for example, weigh less than ten ounces. But filled with air, they're fully rigid components. Most of the weight that's left is in the engine, but even there, with high-temperature plastics and ceramic foams, we've managed to keep the weight to a minimum."

"Astounding." Newell was still staring at the compact package Tom was holding. "And that's how you plan to make your exploratory vehicle? As a fancy balloon?"

"Not exactly," Tom replied as he started across the pavement to the parking area. "If you'll come with me, I'll show you TANC."

The NASA rep's expression grew dubious as they drew near the bright red, high-wheeled vehicle. "It's a good deal smaller than the vehicle called for in the plans your father showed me back at his office."

"This is only a small-scale prototype, for testing and evaluation," Tom replied. "I'd like to be working on a full-size version, but the folks in our accounting department say Swift Enterprises needs to have a firm contract before we go to the next stage."

"Be advised," Newell said as he and Tom came up to the open door of TANC, "your success in getting the contract is by no means assured. Pacific Northwestern Aerospace, Lone Star Dynamics, and Muirhead Development are also presenting entries. So far, though," the NASA rep added with a wintry smile, "only Swift Enterprises has produced any kind of working model."

Tom stowed the folded helicopter in a storage compartment on the vehicle's flank. Then he and Newell climbed aboard TANC, and the vehicle's door swung down. After brief introductions, Rick vacated the front right-hand seat and took a place in the rear. Tom waved Newell to the empty seat, then reclaimed his own place and began fastening the straps and buckles of the safety webbing.

Newell sat down and followed Tom's example. "How do you propose to fulfill the requirements of the contract?" the NASA rep asked as he strapped in.

Tom drew a deep breath and launched into what was by now a familiar explanation. "The Swift TANC utilizes the highly advanced Rover technology. It is capable of taking off from any airfield in the form of a jet plane. Once it reaches the ionosphere, it transforms into a fully operational spacecraft capable of taking astronauts to the moon—or to Mars. On arrival at its destination it changes again into an all-terrain vehicle, allowing the astronauts to move about and explore. The return to Earth reverses the process, right down to landing at any airport. The transformable nature of the craft promises to open up a whole new dimension in space exploration."

"I see," Newell said. He looked out the window at the gaudily painted monster trucks parked to the right and left of TANC, and his dubious expression returned. "And this is—"

"A test of the terrestrial, or all-terrain mode," said Tom smoothly. Just then a huge voice boomed out over both the parking lot loudspeakers and TANC's internal-external monitoring sensors.

"All trucks take your places!"

"I see," Newell said again as TANC's engine started purring, and the vehicle rolled forward out of its parking spot. If the NASA rep's smile had been wintry before, this time it was absolutely glacial.

TANC took its place in a line of monster trucks awaiting their turn at the first event. TANC was up second, right behind the Toledo Tornado.

"They all have such colorful names," Mandy said. "TANC sounds, well, kind of plain next to something like the Abominable Tow-Man."

"Should I have picked something more distinctive?" asked PIPP.

The NASA rep looked interested again. "Is that the vehicle itself talking?" he asked Tom.

Tom nodded. "We've put some very complex artificial intelligence algorithms into the on-board computer." He turned toward the nearest audio pickup. "Don't worry, PIPP. Nobody's going to be judging us on the name."

"That's good, Tom," said the computer. "What is our first event?"

Tom looked over at Rick. "You're the rally expert," he said. "You tell PIPP what to do."

Rick consulted the schedule. "First off, we have the Car Crush," he told PIPP. "The object is to beat everyone else's time going from one end of the row of junk cars to the other."

"A race?" PIPP asked.

"Yeah," Rick said. "Do you see that light bar on the far side of the stadium?"

"I see it."

"Good. When it's your turn, wait until the green light goes on, then get to the far end of that row of cars as fast as you can without having a wreck. Got it?"

"Understood, Rick."

Tom glanced over at Newell, who had been following the conversation with interest. "As you can see," Tom said to the NASA rep, "TANC's AI brain will accept voice commands from authorized crew members."

The NASA rep looked as if he was about to say something, but before he could speak, the voice of the rally announcer came over the stadium PA system.

"Ladies and gentlemen! The Toledo Tornado!"

The yellow lights on the distant light bar

began to tick down one at a time. The monster truck that had been waiting just ahead of TANC started up its engine—a huge, growling noise that sounded through TANC's on-board speakers like a swarm of giant bees. The last light on the bar, the green one, flashed on and the Toledo Tornado leapt forward with a roar.

Clods of dirt flew up in huge arcs behind the Tornado's wheels as it raced toward the long line of junker cars parked side by side in the center of the arena. With a crash the Toledo Tornado drove into the first car. The Tornado's enormous wheels took it up onto the automobile's roof. From there the monster truck rolled forward over car after car, lurching across the uneven surface to the sounds of tortured metal and breaking glass.

The Toledo Tornado rolled over the last car and onto the surface of the arena. A red light came on at the end of the stadium, showing that the truck had ended its run.

The roar of the crowd came into TANC via the onboard speakers, followed by the announcer's voice.

"And now, ladies and gentlemen, a special last-minute entry into the competition—the Swift Enterprises TANC!"

"Stand by," Tom said. "And hold on!"

AT THE FAR END OF THE STADIUM THE LIGHTS once more started flashing: yellow, yellow, yellow—green!

TANC surged forward, pointed directly at the row of junkers. Then, at the last possible second, the Swift Enterprises vehicle swerved to the right.

Still accelerating, TANC pressed on forward—not over but alongside the string of cars. At the far end of the row the vehicle cut hard left and stopped with an abruptness that threw all the passengers forward against the safety webbing.

"PIPP!" Rick exclaimed. "Why didn't you go up and over?"

"You told me to get to this point as fast

as I could, Rick," the AI brain replied. "My analysis of the Toledo Tornado's run indicated that going directly over the parked cars would cause a considerable delay. However, your dismay suggests that I made an incorrect decision."

"It's okay, PIPP," Tom reassured the brain. "You had incomplete instructions. Nobody *told* you to run over the parked cars."

"The score for this event is a best of two, anyway," Rick said. "We'll just have to make good time on our second pass."

"I'll do my best," PIPP promised.

"That's all anyone can ask," Tom said. "Let's go back to the starting line."

The Car Crush went on. Stompomatic followed the Abominable Tow-Man and was followed in turn by Tyrannosaurus Wrecks. One monster truck went down with a broken axle, but the others went on ahead and lined up for their second pass.

"I remember one rally," Rick said as the TANC and its passengers waited a second time for the yellow lights to begin ticking down, "where they forgot to take the springs out of the junkers. Usually they take out the springs and the shock absorbers and flatten the tires to make the cars stay put. But this time they just drove them in and let the trucks have at them. You should have seen it—they had monster trucks bouncing all over the arena."

"Whoops," Sandra cut in. She was watching one of the high-resolution viewscreens showing the arena up ahead. "There go the lights!"

The green light flashed, and TANC roared forward a second time. This time PIPP drove straight at the first car in the line, a station wagon that looked considerably the worse for its recent experiences. The TANC hit the automobile and bounced high into the air, soaring over the parked cars and coming again to the ground just beyond the last car in the line.

"Whew!" said Mandy as the red light came on. "That was quite a ride!"

"Tom said to get over as fast as I could," PIPP said. "I calculated that hitting the first car in line at just the right speed and angle could keep us from wasting time. Did I do something wrong again?"

"No, no," said Tom hastily. "You did it perfectly. A genuine creative solution, one that wasn't programmed in. PIPP, you're great."

"Thank you, Tom. Rick gave me the idea, talking about how those trucks bounced."

Tom glanced over at Peter Newell to see how the NASA representative had taken the trip. To his surprise, the older man was grinning.

"Do you know how many times," Newell

said, "I've gotten stuck on the Washington Beltway en route to a congressional hearing, and how many times I've wanted to do something just like that? I loved it!"

Sandra and Mandy laughed.

"Well, stand by for the next event," Rick told them. "We drive around and around the arena's oval track like a normal race, just to prove that we won't break down."

"PIPP, can you handle that?" asked Tom.

"I'm accessing the encyclopedia file on road races now," said the brain. "Yes, I can handle it."

"Good. Line up with the other trucks, and watch for the start signal. Don't cause any wrecks, okay?"

"Understood."

The race began. As Rick had said, this event was simple and straightforward. PIPP handled the driving, and TANC's superb engineering took care of the rest. Soon the Swift Enterprises entry pulled out in front and kept on running well ahead of the pack.

With PIPP doing the racing, Tom and the others could sit and talk while the other drivers wrestled their trucks around the laps. "Best seats in the house," Rick said. "Tom, when you come through, you *really* come through!"

"I've noticed that Swift Enterprises does a lot of work in transformable vehicles," observed Newell. "The Rover, that portable helicopter, and now your TANC—how exactly do the transformations work?"

"It depends on the device," said Tom. "Some of the earlier transformables relied on mechanical joints. For a space-going vehicle we needed something tougher and more flexible, so we went for servo-controlled superstructure rods underneath a carbon-fiber skin. All of TANC's solid surfaces and strength members are made of laminated ceramic steel to stand up under the heat of reentry."

"What about the interplanetary journey itself?" asked Newell. "You couldn't have several crew members penned up for that length of time inside a cabin not much bigger than, well, than that of a monster truck."

"As I said earlier," Tom replied, "we're talking about a small-scale prototype here. The only thing that's full-scale in this version is the AI brain itself. Besides, PIPP's most important dimensions are the kind you measure in gigabytes, not in cubic feet."

Newell gave another one of his dry chuckles. "Having seen it in action, I'll certainly buy that. But why did you decide to go the AI route in the first place? Wouldn't a normal computer have been more cost-effective?"

Tom shook his head. "I believe it would have been what my grandfather used to call penny wise and pound foolish. In spite of all the robot probes and computer simulations, we won't know exactly what we'll find in interplanetary space until we get there. I wanted something that could bring the astronauts back all by itself even if they were sick or disabled."

He gestured at the race still going on outside the TANC's windows. The Swift Enterprises vehicle remained in the lead. "Look at what's happening right now. We could be incapacitated by Martian canal fever or the Andromedan plague, and PIPP could still drive the bus to get us home."

"And in first place, too," observed Rick after a glance at the scoreboard showed them with a comfortable lead. "Not too shabby for a small-scale prototype."

"I feel kind of bad about that," Tom confessed. "None of the other trucks have nuclear-powered engines or a Polymorphic Integrated Parallel Processor on board. TANC's got an unfair edge."

Rick laughed. "Don't worry, old buddy," he said. "When I signed you up, I told them Swift Enterprises was competing for exhibition only, not for prize money."

"Thanks, Rick," said Tom, feeling relieved. "I guess you know me too well."

"Sure do," said Rick. "You're too modest for your own good sometimes. But TANC's going to put on a great show, anyway. In the last event, the Tug of War, after they do the whole series of eliminations—well, after that we're going to get a shot at the champ. In fact, we're going to tow the champ and the second-place winner *and* the third-place winner, all at the same time."

Mandy looked over at Tom. "Can we do that?"

Tom shrugged, trying to keep up a facade of confidence in front of the man from NASA. I should have known Rick would figure out some way to test everything on board TANC to destruction, Tom thought.

"We won't know until we try" was all he said.

The race ended, not surprisingly, with TANC in first place, and the Tug of War began. The pulls went on for quite some time, with the Toledo Tornado knocking out Hambone, only to be defeated by Stompomatic. Eventually, however, it was time for Tom to test the TANC against the three top finishers: Terror MacFear, Tyrannosaurus Wrecks, and the Gray Ghost.

In the center of the arena the line of junked cars had long since been cleared away. Now Tom directed PIPP to take up a position at one end of the strip. Then the young inventor helped the roadies lead a bridle of heavy chain from an attachment point at the rear of the TANC to towing hitches on the backs of the three other trucks.

"On the signal," Tom told PIPP after he came back from checking the rig, "give a steady pull. Don't jerk or it might hurt something. Then tow those guys around the track. It looks easy enough. The only problems will come if we can't get a good enough grip in the dirt."

"There's the signal for the pull!" Sandra called, looking at her high-res screen.

PIPP had seen it as well. No sound, other than a slight hum and a light vibration, gave any clue that TANC was laboring, however slightly, under the strain. Tom's quick glance at the rear screens, though, showed smoke belching from the exhausts of the other three trucks. A cloud of sand rose into the air around them, and clods of dirt flew up from beneath their tires. Yet neither TANC nor its three challengers had moved an inch.

The man from NASA raised an eyebrow. "Evenly matched?"

Tom checked the readouts on the control panel and shook his head. "I think we've reached the endpoint of friction," he told Newell. "We're grabbing as much as the tires can, but the ground under us isn't hard enough. PIPP, go to ultra-tread mode and keep applying steady pull."

In response to Newell's unspoken question,

Tom explained, "Ultra-tread is the maximum friction version of the tires. They're transformable, too."

"Implementing ultra-tread," PIPP announced as more dust sprayed up into the rear screens.

All at once the whole body of the TANC gave a shuddering jerk and lurched forward toward the far side of the arena, moving fast and still accelerating.

"Oh, no!" Sandra cried. "The tow chain's broken! We're going to hit the wall!"

6

AT THE LAST POSSIBLE MOMENT BEFORE impact, TANC spun around, turning on its own length as it had back in the lab. Now, instead of charging headlong at the wall, the vehicle was accelerating toward the center of the arena.

"Yee-hah!" shouted Rick as TANC hurtled toward the other monster trucks.

Terror MacFear, Tyrannosaurus Wrecks, and the Gray Ghost had been released from the tension of the Tug of War. Now they were roaring at high speed toward the middle of the stadium, trailing the broken tow chain behind them. Before they could go much farther, however, robot arms ending in mechanical claws sprouted from TANC's hull. As the crowd in the arena howled with enthusiasm, TANC grabbed the chains trailing from the three trucks and reversed direction without bothering to turn around.

With all three monster trucks in tow, TANC drove backward three times around the arena's oval track. "Did I do well, Tom?" PIPP asked over the cheers of the crowd. "I didn't have time to ask for advice."

"You did great, PIPP," Tom said. "You saved the day there. Swift Enterprises can be proud of you."

After the award presentations and speeches that marked the end of the rally, PIPP piloted TANC back to its place in the area parking lot. There, at the request of Peter Newell, Tom found himself crawling over and under—and sometimes inside—TANC, with the NASA rep at his shoulder, pointing out the various components and explaining what they did.

The western horizon was flaming with the last rays of the sun before Tom finished telling Newell all about TANC, its special features, and its gadgets.

"About time to head back to the barn," Tom said finally. "Where are Mandy and Sandra?"

"They got thirsty," Rick explained. "Said they'd go off and get something to drink, then come right back. You really ought to put a cooler inside TANC before the next run."

"I know," said Tom. "This is a prototype, remember? I'll check the personnel tracking unit in the cab and see if PIPP can home in on Sandra's locator device."

He glanced over at Newell. "Another big advantage to using AI—with the right implants in the crew's spacesuits, a TANC could locate lost crew members and even run a rescue mission if necessary."

Tom climbed into TANC's cab and turned on the locator screen. The board gave out a ping almost immediately when the tracking unit picked up Sandra's signal. But to his surprise it gave a second ping—that meant another Swift employee was nearby. Tom also picked up the distinctive razz of another tracking unit being used in the vicinity.

"Somebody else is doing some hunting around here," Tom muttered. "And from the sound of the signal, we've also got somebody wearing a bootleg locator, which isn't the genuine Swift Enterprises article. That must be how the thieves were getting stolen parts in and out of the Swift Enterprises grounds without getting caught. I'll need to tell Harlan Ames as soon as we get back home."

Feeling more than a little worried, Tom headed out into the parking lot of the Arroyo Seco Autodrome. The wide expanse of asphalt stood mostly empty by now, and only a few trucks remained. Some of the drivers were doing post-event maintenance on their vehicles, some were loading their trucks onto flatbed trailers, and some were just sitting around, talking.

"Hey, kid, good truck you got," one of the drivers called out as Tom passed. "Thinking about selling it?"

"Nope," Tom replied, his attention mostly on the faint whine of the signal from his locator. He'd gotten Sandra's current position from TANC's board and with PIPP's help had programmed his pocket locator to give a louder signal as he drew closer or a fainter one if he strayed off course.

"Well, if you do think about selling, you could probably get a good price," the man said. "I don't think I've ever seen anything quite like that rig."

"Probably not," Tom replied. "See you later."

Tom moved on. Down by the arena itself, near the business offices and the registration booth, he came to a lighted refreshment area. There the locator's whine rose to its highest pitch. He looked about and without much trouble spotted Mandy and his sister, standing with their soft drinks and hot dogs at a little waist-high table.

"So this is where you went," Tom said. "I was starting to get worried."

"We were getting pretty hungry," Sandra said, "and you were still busy talking to that NASA guy when we left."

"Well, I'm finished now," said Tom. "Are you about done?"

"Sure are," Mandy said. She licked the mustard off her fingers and tossed her empty soda cup into the nearest trash can. "Let's go."

But now Tom hesitated. "Wait a minute," he said. "Sandra, do you see that man over there by the light pole—the guy in the blue shirt?"

Sandra glanced in the direction of her brother's nod. "He certainly does seem familiar," she agreed. "In fact, I'd say that guy was Bill Kane."

Tom nodded. "It sure looks like him. I wonder what he's doing at a monster truck rally?"

Mandy looked puzzled. "Who's Bill Kane?"

"Up until a couple of years ago, he was one of Swift Enterprises' top security people," Tom replied. "But he left a while back because the only way he could have moved up any further was by taking Harlan Ames's job. He was really good—Harlan and Dad wrote references for him."

"So what's he doing here?" Mandy asked.

"Maybe he's a monster truck fan?" suggested Sandra.

Tom frowned. "When there's been a series

of break-ins at the Swift Enterprises ware-houses—break-ins that need someone who's completely familiar with the Swift security arrangements? I wonder."

"Maybe it isn't really him," said Sandra.

"Only one way to find out," said Tom. He left the two girls and strode over to where the man stood. "Hi, Bill."

The man turned to look directly at Tom Swift. "I don't think I know you." To Tom the voice sounded exactly like Kane's.

"Yes, you do. You're Bill Kane."

The other man shook his head. "I'm sure we've never met." Then he turned away. The conversation was clearly over.

Tom walked back to where Sandra and Mandy were waiting. "It's him, I know it," Tom said. "And I could see in his eyes that he recognized me, too. But he doesn't want to admit it in public or be seen talking to me."

"Has he gone bad?" asked Mandy. "Do you think he's involved with the thefts?"

"I don't know," said Tom. "If he were, he'd be more likely to come up with a story about why he's here. I think he's still a good guy but acting under cover—which would imply that there are some bad guys around."

Tom looked out at the gathering shadows of the parking lot. The lights on their tall poles began flickering on, making everything outside the circles of light seem darker by comparison. He remembered the second, unauthorized tracking unit that he'd heard in action—searching for somebody who carried a Swift Enterprises locator device—and said, "I think we should go back to TANC right now."

Mandy and Sandra didn't argue, and the three teens started back toward the monster truck parking area. As they passed between the parked vehicles, two tall men with short, dark hair came out of the shadows between the trucks. Both of the strangers wore gray business suits.

"Tom Swift?" the taller one said. It wasn't really a question. Both of the men flipped open leather wallets containing badges and photo ID cards. "I'm Special Agent O'Malley, FBI. I wonder if we could talk with you briefly." That wasn't a question, either.

"Sure," Tom said. "What can I do for you?"

"We need to talk alone," said O'Malley.

Tom looked at the two girls. "Sandra, Mandy, go on ahead. I'll catch up with you in a minute."

"There have been a number of thefts at Swift Enterprises," O'Malley said when Sandra and Mandy had gone. "We've tracked some of the stolen parts to this arena."

"Here?" Tom could hardly believe his ears. "To a monster truck rally?"

"Some of the monster trucks are being used

as off-road vehicles to run the stolen parts across the Mexican border," O'Malley explained. "But we've found the man we believe is the head of the theft ring. We need you to identify him."

"Sure," Tom said. "Anything to help."

"If you'll come with us ..." O'Malley pointed toward the arena offices, a set of low concrete rooms built into the arcade under the walls near the main entrance. A single light burned near the door, which was stenciled Employees Only. Tom recognized it as the place Rick had gone earlier in the afternoon to enter TANC in the rally.

"If it won't take too long," Tom said. "Otherwise, I ought to call in to Swift HQ first."

"This won't take a moment," O'Malley promised. "Just tell us if you recognize someone."

The two men escorted Tom to the arena offices. Inside, they went down a narrow hallway to the last door on the left, which was labeled Manager. O'Malley opened the door, and Tom saw a cluttered room containing a wooden desk, a swivel chair, and a cork bulletin board covered with scraps of paper impaled on pushpins.

And on the floor an unconscious man.

"Can you identify this man?" O'Malley asked.

Tom knew him, all right. "That's Bill Kane."

"We thought so," said O'Malley as the other agent put a gun at the back of Tom's head.

Acting instinctively, Tom bobbed left and grabbed the gun. He pulled the man forward into a classic shoulder throw, slamming him to the linoleum floor.

But even as Tom moved, O'Malley pressed something cold against Tom's left arm, and Tom felt the brief twinge of an injection from a pneumatic syringe. Tom jerked away and sprinted back down the passageway, trying to reach the outside, fumbling for his personal phone as he ran.

If he could just get out to the parking lot, he'd be okay. If he could just reach the Help button on his pocket phone, he'd be okay.

But neither happened. A black haze swirled up in front of his eyes, and he crumpled to the floor.

7

RICK CANTWELL GLANCED OUT AT THE ARENA parking lot. It was almost full dark by now. Most of the monster trucks had left the Arroyo Seco Autodrome, and the lot was nearly empty.

Tom still hadn't reappeared. Instead, Mandy and Sandra had shown up together. They told Rick that Tom first had spotted former Swift Enterprises employee Bill Kane, and then had been called away by agents of the FBI.

But that had been quite a while ago, and TANC's passengers still sat cooling their heels in the parking lot. Rick looked around the interior of the vehicle. Over by the radar board Sandra and Mandy had their heads together, giggling and comparing notes about school. And in the back of the TANC, Peter

Newell from NASA sat in one of the padded chairs, poring over a notebook full of plans and technical specs. A bright light from the overhead shone down on the top of his balding skull.

The NASA rep wasn't such a bad sort, Rick thought. He just wasn't used to seeing a bunch of kids playing around with a multi-million-dollar piece of gear. Well, if he visited Swift Enterprises more often . . .

But where was Tom? It was night outside, the refreshment stand must have shut down half an hour earlier, and only a half dozen trucks remained in the arena parking lot.

"Tell me again about those two guys who stopped you," Rick said to Mandy.

"They said they were FBI agents and told us they needed to talk with Tom for just a minute," Mandy replied. "They had ID, so I thought it was all right. Maybe Tom's still with them."

"I don't know what to think," said Sandra. "It isn't like Tom to be gone for so long without checking in."

"How do we know he didn't?" Rick asked. "He told us that the communications gear in TANC isn't fully installed. Maybe he called up Swift Enterprises instead. For all we know, he could be waiting for us at the lab."

"Maybe." Sandra sounded doubtful. She stood up and headed for the open door of the

TANC. "There was a pay phone back by the hot-dog stand. If Tom's in some kind of trouble, Dad really ought to hear about it."

After a moment Mandy got up and followed. "You're not going by yourself," she said.

"I'll come, too," Rick said.

Sandra shook her head. "You stay here and hold the fort. Suppose Tom shows up two minutes after we all walk off, and there's nobody here but *him*." She nodded at Newell. "We could wind up chasing one another around the parking lot all night."

"Okay," said Rick. "Mandy, you stick close to Sandra. Make the call to Swift Enterprises and come right back."

At a word from Sandra the TANC's door swung upward. The two girls stepped out into the night, heading for the yellow lights of the refreshment area.

Soon Rick lost sight of them. He sat there, feeling vaguely guilty that he'd let Sandra talk him into staying with the vehicle. Suppose something unpleasant *had* happened to Tom, and the girls had been at least partial witnesses. How safe would they be now?

"You picked a fine time to think about that," he muttered. "Should have brought it up before they left. PIPP, can you follow someone's locator through the on-board personnel tracking unit?"

"Yes, I can," PIPP replied. The brain's quiet voice came from a speaker at Rick's ear, giving the momentary illusion of someone standing invisibly in that spot.

"Great," said Rick. "Keep an eye on Sandra, would you? Watch where she goes and make sure she doesn't run into trouble."

"Understood," PIPP said. "They're near the autodrome, heading around the northeast corner of the building."

"Probably still looking for that phone booth," Rick told the brain. "And for Tom, too, I guess." He paused, then hit his forehead with the heel of his hand. "I'm an idiot, that's what I am. PIPP, can you find *Tom* with the tracking unit?"

"One moment," said PIPP. There was a brief pause. "Yes, I have him."

"Where?"

"Eighty-three and a third kilometers due south," PIPP said. "Approximately."

"What is he doing way out there?"

"About eighty miles per hour," PIPP said. "He's right at the edge of the tracking unit's range. I'm going to lose him any minute now."

Rick bit his lip in indecision. "How about the girls? Are they heading back?"

"Negative," PIPP replied. "Sandra is still moving away from us. Comparing her pace with my stored memories of the autodrome area and assuming she is still with Mandy, I calculate that they have only now reached the refreshment stands."

"How much time do we have before Tom's out of range?"

"His signal is breaking up already," said PIPP. "If we don't shorten the distance, I'm going to lose him."

Rick straightened his shoulders. "Then we don't have any time to waste. Follow Tom!"

"Yes, Rick. Here I go!"

The TANC's powerful headlights came on, burning a path of white light across the asphalt. The vehicle spun in place and pulled out of its spot in the parking area, heading straight for the nine-foot chain-link fence that surrounded the autodrome.

"Stay on the road!" Rick yelled.

"Sorry," PIPP said, and pulled back into the traffic lane. "On the road."

A startled shout came from the rear of the TANC. "Hey, what's going on here?"

It was Peter Newell. The NASA man had been absorbed in his reading. The sudden change in direction had caused two loose-leaf notebooks full of computer printouts and handwritten data to be dumped in his lap.

"We're heading four degrees west of south," PIPP told him. "Plus or minus thirty seconds of arc."

"Stop—let me out."

63

"I'm sorry, sir," PIPP said. "Your voice isn't one of the command frequencies."

"Then *you* stop this thing," Newell told Rick. "I have to get back to Swift Enterprises and finish my report."

"There's no time," said Rick. "Tom's in trouble, and we have to catch up with him before we lose his signal."

Tom struggled back to consciousness like a swimmer forcing his way out of deep water. His body ached all over, and his mouth felt as if it were stuffed with old socks. He tried to lift one hand to his head but found that he couldn't. Somebody had tied his wrists behind him.

O'Malley, he thought. As if the name of the fake FBI agent had been a cue, other memories flooded in: Bill Kane lying bound on the office floor, the struggle, and dark mist rising up around him as the drug hit his system.

That's probably why I feel so bad right now, Tom thought groggily. Whatever O'Malley used to knock me out must have some powerful aftereffects.

Not even the drug's lingering traces in his system, however, could explain why every few seconds the surface underneath him heaved and tilted. When it did, a collection of edges and corners slammed into him hard enough to make his whole body hurt.

With a great effort Tom lifted his eyelids and looked around. The view wasn't encouraging—he was lying on his back in a kind of metal box, open at the top. He could look up and see stars shining among patchy clouds.

He tugged at his hands again. The bonds were very tight. He quit struggling and lay still, trying to collect his thoughts. From the motion and from the engine sounds that gradually made themselves heard over the pounding inside his head, he knew he'd been stowed in the back of a truck. That would explain the huge wooden crates, tied down with wire cables, looming on either side of him.

The truck lurched again, throwing Tom against the sharp corner of the nearest crate. Enough of this, he thought, biting back a gasp as the corner dug into his ribs. He rolled onto his side, his head throbbing afresh at the sudden movement, then pushed himself up onto his knees. In that position his head came above the side walls of the truck's cargo area.

He balanced himself awkwardly, legs apart, and squinted out at the landscape. The countryside he saw was flat and treeless, with a sawtoothed ridge of hills far off on the horizon.

Tom craned his neck and leaned forward as far as he dared to look over the side of the truck. He decided that it would be suicide to jump off. The ground was a long way down and flying by fast. Tom estimated the truck's speed at over sixty miles per hour, and it wasn't even on a road.

Another bump sent him careening off balance. With his hands tied he was unable to catch himself, and he fell with bruising force against the side of one of the crates. Even in the pale starlight he could recognize the logo on the label: Whatever was in the box had been made by Swift Enterprises.

8

RICK CANTWELL SCOWLED OUT AT THE ROAD ahead. Tom was in trouble, he was sure of that, and if his friend was in trouble, then Rick wanted to be taking action and not just watching the road roll up under him.

He clenched and unclenched his fists and wished that TANC had a steering wheel. Maybe then he'd feel as if he was doing something. A steering wheel would give him something to grip, anyway, to keep his hands busy.

PIPP's voice broke into his thoughts. "We have a problem, Rick."

Rick sat up straighter. "What kind of problem?"

"I've lost Tom's signal," said TANC's AI

brain. "I have a mark on his last location, but he's out of range."

"Keep on heading toward that last position," said Rick. "We can't be certain he kept on going in that direction, but it's the only lead we've got."

"No roads headed that way are listed in my data base," PIPP said. "Shall I go overland or go as close as possible on the roads as per your previous instructions?"

"Can you go overland?"

"Yes."

"Then do it." As they jounced over a dune, Rick added, "But don't hit anything!"

"Full sensor scan, collision avoidance running," PIPP said. "Estimated time of arrival at Tom's last known position, thirty minutes from now."

Footsteps sounded on the floor of the TANC as Peter Newell came forward. He had been sitting with the technical documentation in the rear of the vehicle. He lowered himself into the right-hand seat, next to Rick.

"Excuse me," said the NASA representative, "but where exactly do you think you're going?"

Rick frowned at Newell. "Wherever Tom is."

"But I just understood this machine to say that it doesn't know where young Mr. Swift is. I say you should go back to Swift Enterprises and contact the proper authorities. Assuming, of course, that this equipment hasn't malfunctioned and your friend isn't home already."

"Tom wouldn't hesitate to look for me if I were missing," Rick replied. "If he's safe, we haven't lost anything, just a little time running around. But if he's in trouble . . ."

Rick paused, then continued in a quieter voice, "If I were in trouble, Tom would drop everything he was doing to come get me. I won't do anything less for him."

"Such loyalty is admirable," Newell said, "but impractical. Finding your friend is a task for the proper federal agencies. The FBI, for example."

Rick turned his attention back to the readouts on the front panel. They remained disappointingly blank. "NASA wants this machine tested," he said, without looking around. "Well, I'm Tom's chief tester, and I'm testing it."

"Excuse me," said PIPP in the silence that followed Rick's last remark. "A suggestion, if I may."

"Sure, PIPP," Rick said. "Anything out there?"

"It has occurred to me that I could reach Tom's last known location more quickly if I took to the air."

Rick nodded. "Do it."

"I need about a thousand feet of unobstructed, flat terrain for a takeoff," PIPP said. "I'll transform and take off as soon as I find some."

"Now, wait a minute!" Newell interjected. "This is going too far! You can't fly an unregistered, untested aircraft at night. And without knowing where you're going, you can't even file a flight plan."

"I sure can't," said Rick. "But I do have a private pilot's license, with instrument rating. PIPP can handle the flying, and if something goes wrong, I'll take responsibility."

Newell looked at Rick thoughtfully. "You're that certain you're right?"

"Count on it."

"Then I won't interfere," said Newell. The NASA rep gave another of his wintry smiles. "Just be aware that I'll testify—truthfully—at any official hearing that I advised you to return overland to your base."

"Tell 'em whatever you like," said Rick. "But we're going airborne as soon as PIPP finds somewhere we can take off."

TANC continued into the night. Powerful beams from the vehicle's multiple headlight subsystem flooded the highway with light. Beyond the white glare of the headlights, the rocky ground was barely visible. But thanks to TANC's infrared capabilities, a three-dimensional computer graphic of the approaching terrain showed up clearly on the craft's interior monitor screens. TANC rolled over the smaller obstacles and around the larger ones for several minutes, until Rick once again grew impatient.

"PIPP," he said, "where *is* the nearest suitable flat area?"

"State Highway three-oh-two," PIPP replied without hesitation.

"That's the road we just left," put in Newell.

"Can't be helped," said Rick. "Once we're airborne we should be able to make up for the lost time. Okay, PIPP. Head back and run your conversion."

Tom Swift looked again at the crates in the rear of the moving truck. So the story O'Malley gave me really was the truth, he reflected, or part of the truth, anyway.

He wondered what the rest of the truth might be. One thing was certain: He couldn't do anything tied up in the back of a truck. He had to get out while he could still make it back to town.

Tom squirmed and stretched, trying to move his tied hands down to where he could reach his right hip pocket. If he still had his tool kit with him, he could use the minilaser to remove whatever was binding his wrists and then move on from there. At last his fingers touched the pocket, but his tool kit was gone.

"I should have known they'd have searched

me," Tom muttered. The words ended in a gasp as a sharp turn threw him against the side of the truck. He lay for a moment, breathing hard, and waited for his head to stop ringing.

While he rested, the full moon came out from behind the hills and shed its bright, cold light on the truck full of crates. If I can't get out of here, he thought, then I ought to use the light to reconnoiter.

He again pushed himself up onto his knees and shuffled in that position from one of the crates to the next, looking for some clue to what they contained. He was making his way toward the cab of the truck when another jolt knocked him off balance. He toppled and fell, but instead of landing facedown on cold metal, he struck something cloth-covered and relatively warm. A pained grunt from the cloth-covered object told Tom he had fallen onto someone.

The person Tom had fallen on rolled free and in a deep voice asked, "Who's there?"

"Tom Swift. Who are you?"

"You knew me well enough by the refreshment stand," the man said, pulling up his knees and struggling to a sitting position.

Tom looked closely at his fellow prisoner. "Bill Kane?"

"You got it," said Kane. His expression, as he regarded Tom, was not enthusiastic.

"Thanks for messing up my surveillance, bright guy."

"How was I supposed to know you were on a stakeout or something?" Tom said. "For all I know, you go to monster truck rallies every weekend on your own time."

Kane sighed. "Never mind. How did they get you?"

"A couple of guys who claimed to be FBI agents told me that criminals were using the monster trucks to smuggle stolen goods into Mexico. They said they needed me to identify you."

"They've really got some nerve," said Kane. "I'm the one who's an FBI agent! I know who those two punks are, even if I can't prove who their boss is—yet. But they told you the truth about one thing: The stolen parts *are* crossing the Mexican border. I tracked some of the gang to the rally. That's why I was there."

Tom thought for a minute. "Maybe everything O'Malley told me was true. If they spotted me with you, they couldn't tell how much I already knew. They must have figured that if they gave me some obvious baloney, I wouldn't come along."

"You could be right," said Kane. "Did they tell you how the stuff was getting across the border?"

"O'Malley said they were using the monster trucks as off-road vehicles," said Tom.

The young inventor winced as another jolt lifted both him and Bill Kane into the air and slammed them down onto the floor of the truck. "He certainly wasn't kidding about the off-road part, either. Just the same, he and his buddy acted more like rent-a-thugs than criminal masterminds. Does the FBI have any idea who's the real brains of the operation?"

"Our best guess is Arthur Bradshaw," Kane replied. "He's a big player in the international arms market, and he isn't choosy about who buys his wares—or about how he gets them."

"Arthur Bradshaw," said Tom thoughtfully. He shifted his body again, trying without success to find a comfortable position on the metal floor of the truck. His bound arms were starting to cramp behind him, and his hands had already lost much of their feeling. "He was at Swift Enterprises this morning, trying to talk Dad into selling him some of our gear. Dad wouldn't bite."

"It looks like Bradshaw got what he wanted anyway," Kane said. "Have you noticed the labels on these crates?"

Tom nodded. "I saw. Parts for a Tallis Particle Generator. Unless I miss my guess, the same parts that vanished this morning from a Swift warehouse."

"I've heard about the TPGs," said Kane. "Swift Enterprises was going to build those?"

"We'd been thinking about it," said Tom, "but Dad eventually decided not to put the full-power model into commercial production because of the generator's potential for abuse. I wrote a paper on the problem—how the Tallis Cannon asteroid-mining version could be used as a land-based superweapon—for the Department of Defense." Tom sighed. "That paper was classified top secret."

"I know," said Kane. "I read it." The FBI agent looked over at the crate Tom was leaning against. "And so, apparently, did Bradshaw."

"There's something worse," Tom said. "The way O'Malley gave out information like free candy, the way we're tied up back here with the labels on these crates right in front of our noses—Bradshaw hasn't even *tried* to hide things from us."

"I know. He doesn't care what we see."

"That's right," said Tom. "Because we won't be around to testify against him. He's planning to kill us."

9

THE MONSTER TRUCK ROLLED SOUTHWARD across the California desert, bouncing and tilting across the rock-strewn ground. Tom gasped as another jolt slammed him into the side of the crate.

"Are you okay?" Kane asked.

"Nothing that won't keep," replied Tom after catching his breath. "I still want to get out of here."

Kane shook his head. "I've been working on that myself, but whoever tied these knots knew what he was doing."

"Maybe so. But we aren't beaten yet."

With those words Tom lay back on the truck bed and pulled his knees up toward his chest. With his knees tucked against his chin, he began to inch his tied arms down his back. Slowly, slowly, the sinews of his arms and shoulders aching with the effort, he pressed downward until he was able to slip his bound wrists underneath his feet and bring his hands back up in front of him.

He looked down at his hands. Whatever held them didn't look like rope but like something a good deal sturdier. He lifted his wrists to his mouth and tried to untie the bonds with his teeth. No luck.

"I told you," said Kane. "These guys are good at their work. Wait and conserve your strength. Sooner or later someone will untie us, and we'll get our chance."

"We have to be ready for our break when it comes," said Tom. "Let me try to get *you* loose instead."

But Tom's fingers couldn't get a grip on the plasticized material with which Kane was bound. Finally the young inventor sat back with a sigh of disgust. "It's too tight."

"Maybe we could cut it off," said Kane. "There has to be at least one sharp edge somewhere in this collection of boxes."

"The way this thing is bouncing around we'd probably cut our own wrists first," Tom said. "Let me think for a minute. Let's see . . . inside that crate there should be a tube of monomolecular lubricant."

"What's it for?"

"The Tallis Generator has some very tight tolerances," explained Tom. "Some of the places that need lubrication have room for a layer of lubricant only one molecule thick. If we can get to that, breaking out of these bonds is going to be easy."

"If you say so," said Kane. "But how do we get into those crates, with no tools and our hands tied?"

Tom laughed a little under his breath. "Do you think you could help me with my shoelaces?"

"That isn't particularly funny," said Kane.

"I'm not joking." Tom stretched out his leg and shoved his right sneaker under Kane's fingers. "Here, hang on to one end while I pull my leg back. Got it? Good. Now hold steady."

The knot came untied, and the shoelace pulled out into Kane's fingers. "Now what?" said the FBI agent.

"I've been doing some work with microminiature robots," Tom said. "Like the flying pollinators—were you around when I built those?"

"I heard about them," admitted Kane. "Like mechanical bees, weren't they?"

"Sort of," Tom said. "Well, this is similar. These shoelaces are smart—they tie themselves."

"Velcro wasn't good enough for you?"

"Why do things the easy way, when you can

do them the fun way?" Tom replied. "Seriously, a lot of people, folks with advanced arthritis for example, don't have the manual dexterity to use ordinary shoelaces, but if they had a choice they'd still prefer the kind of fit you get only in a lace-up shoe. A self-tying shoelace would let them dress the way they like. Now, what we're going to do, with your help, is get the smart shoelace to thread between the lid and the side of the crate, and then tie itself in the crack. The bulk of the knot should produce enough pressure to lever the lid off."

"That's amazing," said Kane.

"Not *that* amazing," Tom replied. "Sandra and I are still testing the second-generation prototypes. The first ones tended to short out whenever I stepped into a puddle."

"No puddles in here," said Kane. "Let's get started."

Tom and the FBI agent pushed themselves up onto their feet. Kane stood with his back to the crate and braced himself against the sidewall of the swaying truck.

"Something coming up ahead," he announced. "I see lights up there on the horizon."

"On the horizon? That would make it six miles, more or less," Tom said. "We'll be there soon, so here goes."

"Right you are."

Tom and Kane stretched out the smart shoe-lace between them. Then Tom maneuvered about until one end of the lace pressed into the crack between the side and the lid of the crate. When the shoelace was in place, Tom grasped one end between thumb and forefinger and gave the tiny pinch that would start it moving forward—an activity that under normal circumstances would have sent the shoelace threading its way from eyelet to eyelet.

The lace went in slowly, seeking a path. When it was almost all the way in, Tom squeezed the end again. The lace stopped moving. Now if he could just—

"Quick, down!" Kane called.

Tom glanced forward. From what he could see on either side of the cab, he could tell that the monster truck was rolling toward a gate in a high chain-link fence topped with barbed wire. High-intensity floodlights mounted on tall poles lit the ground all around them. Ahead of them Tom could see a giant transport plane standing on a runway. The transport's rear cargo door gaped open, extending like a ramp from the pavement up into the plane's cavernous, red-lit interior.

The monster truck slowed but didn't stop. It drove straight toward the plane. The acrid, sharp-edged smell of hot rubber and jet fuel assaulted Tom's nose, and his ears echoed with the deafening drone of jet engines idling.

He dropped down so that only the top of his head poked above the side of the cargo compartment. A moment later the truck drove up the ramp and into the plane.

Tom heard workers tying down the monster truck to the deckplates of the cargo hold. After the workers had left, the plane's tail ramp lifted with a sigh of hydraulics and swung shut. The jets roared louder, and Tom felt himself sliding backward against the crates as the plane started to take off.

The metal floor of the truck vibrated as the plane gained speed and altitude. Tom swallowed hard to equalize the pressure in his ears and keep his eardrums from popping. Bill Kane did the same.

As soon as the plane reached cruising altitude and leveled off, Tom struggled back up onto his knees and grasped the dangling end of the shoelace. He gave it the double pinch that commanded it to tie a knot. The end slipped out of his fingers and vanished, seeking the lace's other end. A moment later he heard the squeaking noise of nails being forced loose. The top edge of the crate's lid lifted about a half inch.

"Not bad," said Kane quietly at Tom's shoulder.

"We're not through yet," Tom said. He pulled out his shoelace, positioned it at the first eyelet of his right sneaker, and set its tying sequence in motion. As soon as the sneaker was laced and tied, he lay down on his back and pressed both his heels into the gap between the crate and its lid. Then he straightened his legs and pushed upward.

The lid creaked open another inch. Tom repositioned himself and pushed with his legs one more time. The lid tore free on that side.

Quickly Tom stood up and looked around. No one was in sight, and the roar of the jet engines would hide any noise he and Kane might make. Tom saw that monster trucks were parked nose to tail in the forward part of the cargo plane, each truck loaded down with crates and boxes. Some of the boxes had the Swift Enterprises logo stenciled on their sides. Others bore the trademarks of companies such as the Rinaldi Group and UNITECH.

At the sight of the latter trademark, Tom gave a soundless whistle, remembering his own nearly fatal encounter with UNITECH's president, the sinister Xavier Mace. Bradshaw really doesn't care who he gets his parts from, does he, Tom thought.

He reached inside the crate with his bound hands, tearing the foam packing material aside. He groped around, blindly, until his fingers touched the side of a small tube. He drew out the tube and allowed himself to relax for a second, smiling a little. His guess had been right. This was the super lubricant, sealed into its container with a thin layer of metal over the top of the tube.

Tom pushed the seal against one of the exposed nails from the lid of the packing crate. When he pulled it away, a tiny drop of amber liquid welled up from beneath the metal seal. Tom touched the tube of lubricant to the knot binding Kane's hands.

"Okay, now—pull gently," Tom said. "Knots rely on friction to hold, and this stuff should take away the friction."

"Right." Kane began tugging and twisting at his bonds. "They're starting to come loose," he reported a minute later.

"Great," Tom said. "Keep on pulling." He put another drop of lubricant on the knot. Another tug from Kane and the plastic cord slipped entirely free.

Kane rubbed his wrists. "Give that stuff to me," he said. "I'll fix you right up."

The FBI agent took the monomolecular lubricant and put a drop on the cord binding Tom's arms. Tom pulled. His hands were free.

"Great," Tom sad. "Let's get out of here."

"Not so fast," said a nearby voice. The man who had called himself O'Malley was standing there, looking at Tom and Kane. He had a gun in his hand.

"Very impressive," he said. "Now stop right where you are."

10

IN A SWIRL OF DUST TANC CRESTED A SAND dune, then bounced upward and jarred down to the ground. The vehicle ran a few more meters across open ground before leaping over a gully onto the state road. The two-lane blacktop stretched out northward in front of them, empty all the way to the horizon.

"Looks good here," PIPP said. "Want me to convert?"

"Get into the air the quickest way you can," Rick said, "and go find Tom."

"Then I suggest that you both strap in," PIPP said. A few seconds later the electronic brain announced, "Now commencing transformation."

Once again stubby triangular wings extended from TANC's sides, as they had in the Swift Enterprises robotic hangar. The vehicle's nose collapsed and elongated from a blunt truck configuration to the sleek point of a jet. Inside TANC's cab, monitor screens flickered to life.

TANC's speed increased. The vehicle's nose tilted up, and the ground fell away. The huge wheels retracted, clicking into their hidden wells, as the skin of the transformable vehicle extended and covered them over.

The angle of climb increased until nothing showed through the front windshield except a scattering of stars. The numbers on the digital altimeter rapidly increased, and the rate of climb indicator pegged out in the Up direction.

"You young idiot!" gasped Newell as the TANC screamed upward. "We're looping!"

Rick said nothing. He was too busy watching the horizon appear upside down in front of them. Before they could start down on the back side of the loop, the transformable jet made a half roll and steadied into a normal attitude—nose forward, belly down, in level flight heading south.

Rick swallowed. "Ah, PIPP," he said carefully, "what was that all about?"

"I decided to try an Immelmann turn," PIPP replied, its voice sounding calm and relaxed. "Named after Max Immelmann, the

85

World War One ace who invented the maneuver. It's the fastest way to reverse direction when flying, and from your comments, I judged that time might be important."

"It sure is," Rick said. "Just warn me before you do anything that fancy again."

"No problem. Wait a minute—I think I have something."

Rick leaned forward, even though he knew he wouldn't see anything out the windshield except night. "What?"

"We've got more radio range up here," PIPP said. "It's hard to be certain, but I think I've picked up Tom's locator."

"Great! Where is he?"

PIPP delayed a moment before answering. "A lot farther south than I anticipated, and higher."

"Higher? You mean Tom's flying, too?"

"That's right—outside of U.S. airspace, heading south and moving fast. Shall I follow?"

Newell cleared his throat. "I feel I should remind both of you that leaving the country without proper exit papers can have serious consequences."

"So could losing Tom," said Rick. "Keep with him, PIPP. Let us know when you pick up the plane he's on."

"Yes, Rick," said PIPP.

TANC flew onward through the night. The faint green glow from the instrument panel cast weird shadows on everything inside the cockpit. In the eerie half-light Peter Newell's features appeared gaunt and skeletal, and Rick wondered how his own face looked to the NASA rep.

Finally PIPP spoke again. "I have a contact on the radar scope. It matches the position of Tom's locator."

"Sounds good," Rick said. "What's it doing?"

"Leveling off at thirty thousand feet," PIPP replied. "It's a large echo, probably a big aircraft."

"A jetliner?"

"Possibly, but it isn't on a commercial flight path, and it isn't transmitting a civilian IFF."

IFF, Rick knew, meant Identification Friend or Foe. The IFF was a transponder that would send an identifying signal to radar sets equipped to respond to it. Military aircraft, especially, used the identifiers to locate targets and to separate friends from enemies and neutrals.

"No IFF?" Rick muttered, puzzled. "You mean they're not broadcasting anything at all?"

"It's transmitting something," PIPP replied. "But it's neither U.S. military nor civilian. I'm still trying to match it against my library."

"Carry on, then," said Rick. "Tell us when you've got something."

Despite himself, he yawned. The cockpit of

the TANC felt warm, almost cozy, and the hour was past ten P.M. Rick settled back into his seat. The lights on the panel grew dimmer, and his chin settled on his chest. He gave a start and jerked his head up again.

Something's wrong, Rick thought. I shouldn't be this sleepy when Tom's in trouble.

He looked to his right and saw that Newell had already nodded off, his head forward on his chest. Then, despite his struggle to stay awake, Rick's eyes closed as well. He slumped forward against the webbing of the seat harness.

TANC continued its flight southward in pursuit of Tom Swift and the mysterious airplane—but both of the people aboard were unconscious.

On board the cargo plane the phony FBI agent, O'Malley, held his gun leveled at Tom Swift and Bill Kane.

"If it were up to me," O'Malley said, "I'd shoot both of you right here. But it's not up to me. Get out of the truck, very slowly. No sudden moves."

Tom looked at the gun in O'Malley's hand and decided that now was not the time to argue. Carefully, with slow, nonthreatening movements, he climbed out of the monster truck. Kane followed, and the two prisoners stood together next to one of the tall wheels, under the shadow of O'Malley's gun.

O'Malley gave an unpleasant laugh. "At least you've made my problems a little easier," he said. "If you hadn't gotten your hands untied, I would have had to carry both of you down from there myself."

He gestured Tom and Bill Kane forward with his pistol. "Now walk. And don't try anything funny. You don't have anywhere to run to."

Tom nodded and began walking forward through the cargo area of the plane, which looked like a section of tunnel. A car and a half wide, it was lined with soundproofing and lit by a single line of fluorescent tubes running down the center of the overhead. About halfway up the length of the plane a bulkhead split the plane's body into two parts, with the cargo area on one side, and on the other—trouble of some kind, Tom felt sure. In the center of the bulkhead was a door made of polished wood with a brass knocker.

"Okay," O'Malley said when Tom reached the door. "Knock."

Tom raised the knocker and let it fall.

"Come in!" called a voice from behind the door. At a nod from O'Malley Tom twisted the doorknob and gave the door a push. It swung open to reveal Arthur Bradshaw sitting behind a wide desk and working at a portable computer. Tom's personal phone, his binoculars, his electronic notepad, and his mini tool kit lay on the desk beside the computer. Bradshaw glanced up as Tom and Bill Kane entered with O'Malley at their back.

"Here they are," O'Malley said.

"Fine," said Bradshaw. He pulled a pistol from a drawer and laid it on the desk in front of him. "You wait outside. I can handle this myself."

O'Malley withdrew, and Bradshaw turned to the two prisoners.

"I believe we all know one another," he said.

"Arthur Bradshaw," Kane replied. "I thought I might find you behind all this."

"Indeed." Bradshaw smiled, reminding Tom of nothing so much as a well-dressed shark. "And you see, you were right. But this encounter is truly an unexpected pleasure. And young Tom Swift and I have already met—this morning at his robotic hangar."

The arms dealer picked up the thin-film binoculars and began to play with them. "When my men reported you were talking with young Mr. Swift here at the rally, I knew I couldn't wait. Who knows what you might have told him? So I had to take you both out of circulation. Permanently. How unfortunate that none of your friends at the bureau believed you about me, Mr. Kane. You were working on your own time, without backups, and there's no way to transmit your findings now."

90

"You won't get away with this," Kane said.

"Oh, yes, I will," said Bradshaw. "In fact, I have. But I do have an offer of sorts for you, particularly for young Mr. Swift."

Bradshaw twisted to look directly at Tom. He tapped a manicured fingernail against the thin-film binoculars. "A nice piece of gear. Your own design, I suppose?"

Tom didn't answer.

Bradshaw nodded to himself. "I rather expected that, but it doesn't matter. Your touch is unmistakable. If these go into general production, I'll have one of my subcontractors buy a hundred thousand of them at least. Meanwhile, since you've fallen so fortuitously into my hands, we two have some serious business to discuss."

He set the binoculars back down with the rest of Tom's equipment and picked up the pistol. "I read that excellent report of yours on the Tallis Cannon. So did one of my many clients. He now wishes to have a cannon of his own. With your help, plus the parts here in this plane, I can build one for him."

Tom shook his head. "I couldn't be a party to something like that."

"Oh, yes, you could," Bradshaw said mildly. "You have a choice, Tom Swift. You can help me or you can die."

IF YOU HAVE THE PARTS AND THE PLANS," countered Tom, "then what's the point of endangering yourself by kidnapping me?"

"I want your knowledge," said Bradshaw. "You're an idealist, like your father. I suspect that when you wrote about converting the Tallis Particle Generator to a lethal weapon, you left out a vital step or two just in case the information came into the wrong hands. Although I don't doubt—and neither should you—that my workers could build the cannon themselves if the need arose, it would be easier if you handled the construction."

Tom nodded thoughtfully. He'd been expecting something like this ever since he'd seen the labels on those crates. "And if I say no?"

"Then I'd be forced to let you go," said Bradshaw. The arms dealer paused, then added, "You'd have to walk home, of course. From here."

"You'd drop the kid out of an airplane?" Kane exploded. "Even for you, that's reprehensible!"

Bradshaw smiled at the FBI agent. "Do try to remember, Mr. Kane, that young Mr. Swift is not absolutely essential to this operation. And you, my friend, are far less essential than he."

The arms dealer pressed a button on his desk. A moment later another man stuck his head into the office.

"Tie these two up," Bradshaw said. "Do a better job than last time. And put a guard on them."

The man looked at Tom. "Huh. This one's just a kid."

"Idiot!" Bradshaw yelled, his face going red with sudden anger. "That isn't 'just a kid'! That's *Tom Swift*. Tom Swift would be dangerous welded into an iron cage! I say watch him. Watch him carefully. If he twitches, kill him instantly!"

As suddenly as Bradshaw's anger exploded, it vanished. He turned back to Tom. "Well," he said, as if he'd never raised his voice, "what do you say? Will you work for me?"

Tom thought fast. If he said no, Bradshaw

might kill both him and Bill Kane. But if he pretended to go along, he could learn more about Bradshaw's operation and still watch for a chance to get away.

"I don't seem to have a choice," Tom replied, mentally crossing his fingers. "I'll do whatever you want."

"That's more like it," Bradshaw said. "I'll see you again on the ground." He stood and walked out through a door leading farther forward in the aircraft.

"What do you think?" Tom muttered to Kane out of the side of his mouth.

"Don't do it!" Kane whispered back. "Do you know what he could do with—"

"Shut up, you two," said the man who had come in answer to Bradshaw's signal. "Put your hands behind your backs and cross your wrists."

Tom and Kane did as they were told. Tom felt his hands being bound. Then a black hood was slid over his head. Strong hands pushed him into a facedown position on the carpeted deck of the office and tied his ankles. He tugged at the plastic cord binding his wrists, testing its strength. A second later he heard the sound of a pistol being cocked.

"Don't move," a voice said. "I see what you're doing, and I don't like it."

Tom made no more effort to test his bonds. He lay for a long time without moving, getting stiffer and stiffer. Even through the office carpeting, the deck of the aircraft was cold, and the powerful engines made it vibrate uncomfortably. At last Tom did the only logical thing: He willed himself to relax and went to sleep.

He came awake to the sound of servomotors whining as flaps extended from the airplane's wings. Then a thump sounded beneath him as the landing gear extended. The airplane came down with a bump, and Tom felt inertia sliding him forward as the plane slowed. At last the plane came to a stop, and the noise of the engines died.

"All right, you two, on your feet."

Tom felt the cords that bound his ankles fall away—cut, he supposed. Someone grabbed his elbows and pulled him upright. He could no longer feel his hands, and his shoulders were painfully cramped.

With the black bag still over his head, Tom was guided down a passageway to a ramp, then down to what finally felt like hard ground underfoot.

Someone stripped the hood from his head. Tom looked around and saw that he stood on an airfield with Bill Kane beside him. Behind them the airplane they'd just left loomed up as high as a five-story building. From the plane's size and shape Tom recognized it as a C-5A Galaxy—a giant military transport aircraft. A half-dozen of Bradshaw's hirelings stood close by.

The sky above the C-5A was starting to grow light with the first hint of dawn, but a scattering of stars remained visible. Those aren't northern hemisphere constellations, Tom realized. We must have come a long way—to South America, maybe.

"Come on, you two," said the man who had hustled Tom and Bill Kane off the C-5A. "The boss wants to see you."

The two prisoners were marched between two armed men toward the huddle of concrete buildings constructed beside the airstrip. As the sky grew lighter, Tom saw that an expanse of rugged desert surrounded the base on all sides. Off in the west a dark, shadowy mass rose above the horizon—a line of clouds, perhaps, or distant mountains.

The man motioned Tom and Bill Kane into one of the buildings. Bradshaw was already there, waiting beside a stack of crates bearing the Swift Enterprises logo.

"I hope you'll find everything you need," Bradshaw said. "I want you to construct a Tallis Cannon as quickly as you can. There's no point in attempting to escape. You're hundreds of miles from any kind of civilization, in the middle of a desert, and there's no food or water away from this base. You wouldn't last a day on foot."

Bradshaw regarded Tom for a moment, as if considering something. Then he went on. "Just in case you're about to try something noble and self-sacrificing, without a thought for your own safety, I have something else to show you. To guarantee your good behavior, you might say."

The arms dealer gave a signal, and two men with rifles slung on their backs came forward from the back of the building, escorting a pair of girls between them. With a gasp of dismay Tom recognized Mandy and his sister.

"Mandy! Sandra! Are you all right?" he shouted. "How did they get you?"

Mandy broke away from the men escorting her and ran forward. "Oh, Tom, Tom, what have they done to you?" she cried as she collapsed against Tom and began sobbing on his shoulder. Between sobs she whispered quietly in his ear, "Sandra's carrying a Swift locator. Do you still have yours?"

"It's built into my belt buckle," Tom whispered back. "But I'm not going to leave without you and Sandra."

"Don't worry about us," Mandy whispered. "Get away if you can, and bring back help." Then once again she began crying and screaming.

"You see?" Bradshaw said as one of his men pulled Mandy off Tom and took the two girls away. "I nabbed them just before they got to the phone booth back at Arroyo Seco. No one has any idea where they are—they never had a chance to make a call. So if you want to keep your sister and her friend healthy, Swift, do what I say. Build me a Tallis Cannon." The arms dealer looked pointedly at his watch. "You have six hours."

Bradshaw withdrew through the same door as the one through which the girls had been taken. The armed man who had escorted Tom from the plane cut the bands on his wrists and departed, leaving Tom and Kane alone with the crates and boxes.

Tom walked around the edges of the room, examining it and swinging his arms as he walked to get the blood flowing back into his hands. The room had no windows; all the light came from banks of fluorescent tubes high overhead. There were only two doors, both made of iron, with no knobs or keyholes showing on the inside. Even the hinges, Tom noted, were on the outside of the building.

Tom turned back to Bill Kane. "What do you think?"

Kane shook his head. The FBI agent put his finger to his lips and pointed around the room. Tom followed Kane's gesture and saw that security cameras and microphones were spaced around the room near the ceiling, at least twelve feet above the top of Tom's head.

Tom shrugged and began pulling the crates

of parts for the Tallis Cannon to a location near a workbench along one bare wall. Kane moved to join him at his work.

"Don't trick yourself into thinking Bradshaw will let us go, Tom," the FBI agent whispered as the two of them bent over a box, lifting out an amplified power coil. "He's going to wait until the cannon is almost done, then get rid of us and let his research staff finish it."

"I'm not surprised," murmured Tom. But Bradshaw may be, he added to himself. A cannon isn't the only thing you can build with the parts of a Tallis Particle Generator. "Do you think the girls are safe?"

"For the moment," Kane replied. "Dead hostages are no use to anyone."

An intercom speaker crackled. "Get to work, gentlemen. You have five hours and fifty minutes."

At that moment one concrete wall cracked and smashed inward. Daylight poured into the hole, making lines in the floating cloud of concrete dust. It was the Swift Enterprises TANC in its terrestrial mode, smashing through the thick wall as if through plywood.

TANC's driver-side door swung upward. "Climb in, Tom!" came a voice over the outboard speakers. "We're getting out of here!"

12

SANDRA SWIFT AND MANDY COSTER WERE SIT-
ting behind barred doors on the concrete floor
of an empty cell. It was lit by fluorescent
tubes encased in plastic shields on the ceiling.
Except for the girls' own breathing, the only
sound was the nearby whine of an air condi-
tioner with a condenser rapidly going bad.

"Now what?" Mandy asked. "I'm sure Tom
can find a way to escape and get help, but
I'm not so certain how useful we're going to
be to Bradshaw once Tom's gone."

"Too useful," Sandra replied. "But I'm not
planning to stick around and let Bradshaw
use me to make Dad jump through hoops.
That man wants the latest Swift Enterprises
technology, and he doesn't care how he gets

it. Besides," she added, "Bradshaw was smart enough to take my locator before he locked us in here. Tom wouldn't know where to start looking for me if he could."

"Looks like we have to rescue ourselves," agreed Mandy. "But how are we going to do it?"

Sandra smiled. "Bradshaw and his guards will be busy watching Tom. He won't waste his time worrying about a couple of harmless girls safely locked up in a cell. So we'll let Tom provide the diversion."

A heavy thump, more felt through the walls than heard, hit their prison cell. The lights flickered, went out, then came back on at half their previous intensity.

"And unless I miss my guess, that's Tom making his move right now."

It was Mandy's turn to laugh a little, in spite of their predicament. "Or maybe Rick. Massive destruction is more his style."

"You said it," Sandra replied. She turned up the bottom hem of her shirt and began picking at it with her fingernails. "Here we go," she said. "I thought I could find a loose stitch somewhere."

She began to unravel the edge of the garment. Soon she had several feet of thread. "Take hold of the end of this string," she told Mandy, "and don't lose it."

Mandy complied. Sandra pulled off her

watch and tied it onto the end of the thread she had taken from her blouse. Then she stuck her hand through the barred door of the cell and began to swing the makeshift plumb bob back and forth like a pendulum.

"What are you trying to do?" Mandy asked.

"See down there in the passageway? To the left, about five feet away? There's an electric eye. If I can break the beam with this weight . . ." The watch was really swinging now. "And there it goes."

Somewhere outside the cell, a shrill alarm began to sound. Sandra reeled the thread and the watch back in, stuck them into her pocket, and took a seat against the far wall.

Not a moment too soon. The outer door flew open, and two men with drawn pistols came running in.

They seemed surprised to see the two girls still safely locked in the cell. "What are you— Oh, forget it," one of them said.

"What's going on?" Sandra asked, her voice innocent.

The two men turned to leave. "Malfunctioning piece of—" one of them muttered to the other as the outer door swung shut behind them.

"Places for act two," Sandra said. She went back to the cell door, unrolled the little ball of thread, and began swinging the weight again. The moment it broke the beam, the alarm sounded again. Once more, Sandra reeled it in and took her place against the wall. The guards opened the outer door, looked in, went to the cell, and shook its door.

"I told you," the first guard said to his companion. "The alarm's on the fritz again." They left.

"Once more, with feeling," Sandra said. She repeated her actions with the thread and the watch a third time. The alarm started, but this time no one opened the outer door. After a few minutes the alarm stopped.

"Now." Sandra swung her homemade plumb bob for the fourth time. This time, when it swung across the beam of the electric eye, no alarm sounded.

Sandra looked satisfied. "They turned it off at the main control board," she said. "I thought they would. Now's when the fun begins."

Bending down, she pulled lightly at the instep of her right sneaker. The lacing gave a twitch and slithered free. She set the end of the lace to the keyhole of the lock and gave the lace a pinch. The lace began squirming into the lock like a miniature snake seeking its hole.

"It's not a proper skeleton key," she observed. "But it'll do."

"The electronic shoelace! You showed it to me last week. I thought it was silly, didn't I? Sorry, Sandra. I should never underestimate you or Tom. But how come you know so much about locks?" Mandy asked.

Sandra smiled. "Oh, just one of the many odd jobs I do around Swift Enterprises. We needed to secure our facilities, so I studied every make of lock on the market. And here we go." The lock clicked slightly, and the door swung open a fraction of an inch. The shoelace slid out of the lock, and Sandra caught it before it could drop to the floor.

"Let's go," she said. "As they say, Fortune favors the bold—so let's work on being fortunate."

"I'm right with you," said Mandy. They left the cell, and Sandra shut the door behind them. Together they walked to the outer door.

"Just as I thought," Sandra said after a moment's examination. "They're relying too much on their alarm panel." She did something with the shoelace to a part of the door-frame and was rewarded by a shower of sparks. The door swung open.

"Well, that kills one shoelace," Sandra observed. "I'll have Tom make me another when we get back."

The opening door broke the photoelectric beam, but just as Sandra had hoped, no alarm sounded. Moving silently, the two girls tiptoed down the passageway. Around a corner they came to a control room opening off the corridor. The two guards sat inside, watching a monitor screen. But instead of showing the holding cells, the screen showed the surface of the base. A cloud of smoke blew across the picture, and Sandra smiled as a familiar shape came barreling out of the haze—the Swift Enterprises TANC.

"Our life just got easier," she whispered to Mandy. "Here comes the cavalry to the rescue right now."

When TANC first crashed through the wall of the building, Tom could hardly believe his eyes. But he didn't stop to question his good fortune.

"Here's something I bet Bradshaw *never* expected!" he exclaimed. "Give me a hand, Bill. Let's get these boxes on board for evidence. PIPP, open up your cargo bay."

The storage compartment on TANC's side swung open. Tom and Kane loaded the parts for the Tallis Cannon into the storage compartment, right behind the folded ultralight portable helicopter.

"We're going to have company," PIPP said as they threw the last box into the hold. "Armed men running this way."

"Get aboard," Tom called to Kane. With Kane following, he swung up the ladder to TANC's cab. "Shut the door, PIPP," Tom ordered as he climbed. "We have to get the girls."

The door swung down. Tom saw that Rick Cantwell was sitting in the driver's seat. Good old Rick, thought Tom, and then looked closer. His friend was unconscious, with a faint blue tinge to his face and lips. In the next seat Peter Newell, the man from NASA, was also out.

"Oh, no," Tom said. "PIPP, what's wrong?"

"I don't know," said the electronic brain. "They haven't spoken in several hours. Is that not normal?"

"Hmm," Tom said as Rick began to stir and mutter. "What were you doing at the time?"

"Flying down here after you, Tom."

"Was the cabin pressurized?" Kane asked. He was kneeling beside Newell. "This looks like oxygen starvation to me."

"No, the cabin wasn't pressurized," PIPP admitted. "That wasn't something I was told to do."

Tom drew a deep breath. There's no point in getting angry, he reminded himself. PIPP's only a computer, after all. It doesn't have to breathe, and it's still learning how to think.

"PIPP," he said, "from now on keep the air in the cabin within one percent of normal earth atmosphere at sea level."

As he spoke, armed men broke into the warehouse through both doors. "Back out!" Tom shouted to PIPP. "Get us out of here!"

The men began firing small arms at TANC.

But the carbonite skin of the vehicle was tough—it was designed to withstand micro-meteorites at rocket speeds. The bullets bounced off. TANC hurtled backward fast enough to knock Tom and Bill Kane off their feet, then spun in place and drove off to the northeast at high speed.

"Wow, what a trip," Rick said, coming fully awake. "Where are we?"

"In the Catamarca," PIPP replied. "A desert in northwest Argentina, bordering on Chile. Several mountain ranges cross the Catamarca, of which the Andes form the western border."

"Thanks, PIPP," Tom broke in. "We don't have time for the whole encyclopedia entry. We have to rescue the girls. But first, we're going to make sure Bradshaw can't take them anywhere else. Get us to the airfield."

"Going to the airfield now," PIPP replied. TANC spun again and headed back toward the field where the giant C-5A still waited amid a host of smaller planes. "Head for the Galaxy," Tom said. "Get close enough so we can attach your tow chains to the landing gear."

"Will do," PIPP replied. TANC roared right up the runway, atomic-powered wheels pounding on the tarmac, up under the shadow of the wings of the C-5A. The vehicle spun to a halt near one of the wheel clusters.

"Open the door, PIPP," Tom ordered. "I

have to go outside for this. Rick, want to help?"

"What are you doing?" shouted Peter Newell, now conscious in the passenger seat. "Get us out of here!"

"Let Tom be," advised Kane. "I've seen this kid in action before, and I can promise you, it won't be dull."

TANC's door eased open. Tom and Rick piled out and ran around to the rear of the vehicle. Tom unreeled the heavy chain that was still attached there from towing the monster trucks. Together they carried the chain around one of the pylons supporting the huge tires and hooked the chain to itself in a loop. Then they ran back and clambered into the driver's compartment just as more guards arrived on the scene, this time firing submachine guns.

"Close the door, PIPP," Tom said. "Never mind those guys. Start up slow and steady, just like in the arena."

"Slow and steady," confirmed PIPP. "You do realize there is a significant risk of breakage to the C-5A if I persist in this course of action?"

"Breakage is part of the general idea," said Tom. "Go to ultra-tread and pull as hard as you can."

"Implementing ultra-tread," announced PIPP. "Here we go." The TANC eased forward until all the slack came out of the chain. "It's starting to move."

"All right, everybody," Rick called out. "Make a wish!"

Rick's reference to pulling apart a wishbone was right on the mark. The hydraulic supports of the giant transport plane had already started to bend.

A little more power from TANC, and the C-5A's landing gear snapped off. Released from the Galaxy's anchoring weight, TANC sprang forward just as the giant cargo plane tilted and began to collapse—with TANC and its passengers in the way beneath it.

BACK IN THE UNDERGROUND PRISON THE TWO guards had their attention fixed on the screen. Sandra looked at Mandy, put her finger across her lips, and motioned at her friend to follow her past the open doorway of the control room. They walked on to where the passageway dead-ended in an unlocked door leading to a bank of elevators.

Sandra turned to Mandy. "Want to push the button?"

"I don't know," Mandy said doubtfully. "Judging by the way the lights have been flickering, we could get trapped in there."

"We may have to take that chance," Sandra replied. "I don't see any stairs. Give me a hand here. Let's take a peek at the elevator shaft."

Sandra stood on one side of the elevator doors and Mandy on the other. They put their fingers in the slight gap where the two doors met and pulled. Slowly the doors eased open.

Sandra looked inside. "There we go. A ladder."

The elevator car was at the top of the shaft. But Sandra's guess had been right—a service ladder of gray-painted metal ran flush with the wall along the right-hand side of the door. With the outer doors open, the girls could see that the front wall separating the shaft from the corridor was made of concrete over ten inches thick.

"Let's go up," said Sandra. "There should be an access hatch in the bottom of the elevator car and another at the top. We can go through the car and out the top of the shaft."

She swung over onto the service ladder and began climbing. Mandy followed a second later, and the doors slid shut behind them. The shaft wasn't totally dark. Illumination came from the top but was mostly blocked by the bulk of the elevator car. Still, enough light came past so that they could see their way upward.

They had gone about halfway when a click and a whine above them alerted them to danger. "Oh, no!" Mandy exclaimed. "The elevator's coming down. We're going to be crushed!"

The descending bulk of the elevator filled the entire shaft. "Quick!" said Sandra. "The next floor up!"

She didn't waste breath explaining further but scrambled up the next few rungs of the ladder to the gap where the thick wall formed a ledge between the outer sliding doors and the empty shaft. There was just enough room for her and Mandy to squeeze in side by side, with their faces pressed against the closed doors and their backs to the elevator car as it came down.

"If it stops on this floor, we're in trouble," Mandy said.

But the car slid past them, its inner doors remaining closed, and continued on its journey downward.

Mandy let out a sigh. "That was close."

"We're not out of the woods yet," Sandra told her. "The chances are that whoever was in that elevator was going down to check on us, and when they find us gone, the alarm bells are going to be ringing all over this base."

"So what are we going to do?"

"First, let's pry these doors open and get off this ledge. Then we can think about what to do next."

Working the sliding doors apart was harder

to do standing on the narrow ledge than it had been back in the hall. But the two girls braced themselves against each other and against the concrete sides of the door, and pulled with all their strength. Finally they succeeded in forcing the sliding doors apart and half stepped, half stumbled out into another empty passageway.

"That's better," said Sandra. She looked around to get her bearings. "We know Tom's somewhere around here, and so's TANC. Let's link up with them. Once we get to the surface, that should be easy."

"Right," said Mandy. "Just head toward where all the large valuable objects are falling over, blowing up, or bursting into flames."

The girls began jogging down the corridor. This one ended in a set of double doors fitted with windows. Peeping through the windows, they saw what looked like some kind of control room. It was empty.

"Whatever Tom is up to, it must be keeping most of Bradshaw's people busy on the surface," Mandy commented.

"We're pretty close to the top ourselves," said Sandra. "Let's see what's on the other side of this room."

She pushed the door open. The inside of the control room was fitted out with monitors, dials, and levers. An airtight door led away

113

to the left. Several gas masks in plastic cases hung from pegs on the wall.

"Nothing here," said Sandra, heading for the far door.

"Wait a minute," called Mandy. She had paused beside one of the monitor screens, and Sandra noticed that Mandy's face had gone pale. "Sandra, come take a look at this."

Sandra hurried over to the bank of monitors. But before she could look at the screen Mandy had indicated, all the lights in the room began flashing at once, and a voice boomed out over the loudspeaker.

"Prisoner alert, prisoner alert. Two females escaped from cellblock H."

With its support pylon snapped in two by TANC's pulling, the C5-A Galaxy toppled sideways. The giant transport jet's descending shadow blanked out the sky.

"PIPP!" Tom shouted. "Get us clear!"

The engines crescendoed as PIPP fed them even more power. TANC jumped forward ten feet and then stopped. They had not yet cleared the shadow of the falling transport.

"What's happening?" cried Rick.

"Swift, get us out of here," said Peter Newell through tight lips.

The crashing Galaxy was picking up speed as it fell. All eyes were on Tom, who was staring frantically at the glowing readouts on the board in front of him.

"Of course!" said Tom, smacking himself in the head with the palm of his hand. "TANC! Release the tow chain immediately and get moving."

TANC roared out from beneath the belly of the huge transport and screamed forward across the tarmac just as the plane went all the way over. The tip of the C-5A's enormous wing scraped across TANC's roof and smashed into pieces against the ground.

TANC sped on across the landing field. In its wake the great plane lay on one side like a wounded whale, ruptured tanks bleeding a slick of fuel across the runway.

"That one's down," said Rick. "But what about all the little stuff? They've still got plenty of things here that can chase us home."

"I'm working on it," said Tom. "PIPP, do you see that fuel truck over there?"

"I see it, Tom," said PIPP.

"Good. If the bad guys don't have gas, they can't take off. So let's give it the old monster truck smash."

"No problem," said PIPP. "Here we go." The vehicle spun again and headed for the tanker parked at the side of the airfield. PIPP brought TANC up beside the truck and pushed against it.

Just as the fuel truck started to tip over, a

rocket-propelled grenade flew out of the desert, trailing an arc of smoke. The grenade missed TANC but hit the fuel truck, and with a tremendous explosion the tanker turned into a ball of flame. A column of black smoke headed skyward.

Thanks to its heat-resistant construction, TANC was unscathed, but the passengers inside flinched at the blazing wreck just in front of their faces. Tom shielded his eyes, but while he did so, his mind raced to the next step in their escape.

"If we can cover the runway with fuel and set it on fire," he said, thinking aloud, "that ought to take care of the rest of the planes without our having to go outside."

"Just make sure you don't get us, too," said Newell.

"Don't worry," said Tom. "TANC is designed to take the heat of reentry. A kerosene fire won't bother us a bit. PIPP, can you handle spreading the flames around?"

"Of course, Tom," said the AI brain. TANC began to push the blazing wreck across the airfield. The truck spilled out a trail of flaming kerosene as it went. When the flames touched the lake of fuel spreading out from the downed C-5A, that fuel also ignited with a tremendous whoosh. The damaged plane blazed up like a torch.

"Arthur Bradshaw has certainly annoyed

me a great deal from time to time," Kane said, "but I never expected to see his whole operation leveled like this."

"It isn't leveled," Tom said. "This is just going to slow him down a bit while we look for Sandra and Mandy. PIPP, can you pick up the signal from Sandra's locator?"

"Yes, I can, Tom. Shall I home in on her?"

Tom nodded. "Let's do it, then get out of here and head for home. Mom and Dad are probably more than a bit worried by now."

"I have Sandra on the scope," PIPP announced. "Coming up on screen three in front of you."

Tom studied the display for a moment. "Underground?"

"So it appears."

"What are we supposed to do now?" asked Rick. "Get out and dig?"

"Wait a moment," PIPP said. TANC stopped in place. A previously blank display screen lit up with a list of rapidly scrolling numbers. PIPP began counting aloud. "Five, four, three, two, one, *now.*"

On the last word the burning Galaxy on the runway exploded with a thunderous roar.

"How did you do that?" Newell asked, sounding impressed.

"I calculated the rate of burning and the size, location, and potential of the main port-side fuel tank," PIPP replied. "The rest was simple."

"So?" asked Rick. "Let's get going, people. They're still shooting at us."

"Echoes coming back now," PIPP replied.

A second later the vehicle started up. "I put down the seismographic sensors," PIPP explained. "I had to be standing still to do that. I knew that a massive explosion would give me an echo picture of any underground structures. As I surmised, what we see on the surface is only part of Bradshaw's Catamarca base. There's a huge buried complex here, and Sandra is down there in it."

"Can you get inside from here?" Tom asked.

"Affirmative, Tom," said PIPP. TANC sped away to where a rocky outcrop dominated the arid scenery. The vehicle didn't swerve but instead crashed directly into the face of the stone. What had seemed to be solid rock broke away. TANC's passengers found themselves in a large underground passageway lit by glowboxes set along the ceiling.

"Let's go," Tom said. "The personnel tracking unit puts Sandra right ahead."

Down the corridor they went, halting at a set of double doors. "The unit indicates that the girls are on the far side," PIPP said. "Shall I go in?"

"Yes," said Tom. "Take it low and slow.

We can't be sure of exactly where they're standing."

Moving gently now, TANC pushed against the doors. They opened for the massive vehicle, and PIPP guided the TANC into another of the large, dimly lit warehouse rooms that Bradshaw had spaced around his hidden base.

Tom saw with relief that the tracking unit had been correct. The two girls were safe inside, sitting on the floor with their backs against the far wall.

"Oh, Tom!" Mandy called out, her voice carried into the cab by the TANC's external microphones. "Thank goodness you're here! I was so worried!"

"We're tied up!" Sandra cried. "Come get us loose!"

"PIPP, open the doors," Tom said. "We have to go untie the girls."

But the winglike doors of the TANC remained closed.

"The girls are here," Tom repeated. "PIPP, open the doors so we can bring Sandra and Mandy inside."

"I'm sorry, Tom," PIPP said. "I'm afraid I can't allow you to do that."

PIPP!" TOM SHOUTED. "I'M NOT KIDDING—open the doors!"

"No, Tom. I can't do that."

"Please, Tom!" came Sandra's pleading voice from the dimly lit room. "Come out and untie us!"

"PIPP," said Tom steadily. "You'd better have a really good explanation for this. I can still unplug you and put TANC under manual control."

"You told me not to let the atmosphere inside the vehicle differ by more than one percent from normal sea level," PIPP said. "If I open the door, the atmosphere will be different."

Don't get angry, Tom reminded himself yet

again. PIPP is still learning. It doesn't know any better.

"If you mean the pressure will drop because we're up above sea level, then don't worry about it. You can open the door."

"No, Tom." This time it was the AI brain's voice that sounded like that of a teacher instructing a backward student. "The atmosphere in this room contains a high concentration of dimorphic xenotoxin, a highly poisonous gas. There's no dimorphic xenotoxin in normal sea level air. Nor has our forcible entry caused the gas to dissipate—dimorphic xenotoxin is heavier than air."

"That can't be," Rick said. "Look, the girls are out there, and they're doing fine. Your sensors must be messed up."

"I've checked my sensors, Rick. They are functioning perfectly, and I won't open the doors."

"Hold on," said Tom. "I have an idea. Mandy," he called over TANC's external speakers. "What color bathing suit did you wear on our date last Friday?"

"There's no time for that, Tom!" Mandy cried. "Get out and untie us before Bradshaw comes back!"

"I think I know what you're doing," Rick said. He picked up the microphone link to the outside. "Sandra, what did you and Kathy Taylor call me in third grade?"

"That's not important right now!" Sandra cried. "Please make Tom open the door!"

"She didn't meet Kathy Taylor until junior high," Rick muttered. "I don't know what's going on, but those aren't our Sandra and Mandy out there."

"PIPP, take us out of here!" Tom called out to the AI brain. "It's a trap!"

"You are undoubtedly correct," PIPP replied. "But I recommend that we not leave."

"Don't be difficult, PIPP," Tom said. "Keep the doors shut the way you wanted to, but get us out of here."

"If you insist, but my sensors indicate two sets of light footsteps approaching this chamber at a run. It might be advisable to wait a few seconds longer and see who emerges from that door in the far wall."

"Thirty seconds," said Tom "Then we're gone."

Tom watched the chronometer on TANC's control panel as it ticked down toward the mark. His right hand hovered near the manual override. But the count still had a good ten seconds left to go when the far door opened and two girls in gas masks ran out. Except for the masks they were identical to the other Sandra and Mandy. The two masked figures ran past their unprotected twins and started banging on TANC's passenger-side door.

"It really is them this time," said Rick. "It has to be. The others are probably just decoys—dressed-up mannequins with microphones in them. They told us they were tied up, so we never expected them to move."

"Maybe," said Tom. "But Bradshaw is tricky enough to run a double-blind on us. These girls might be decoys, too—assassins, maybe, with orders to take over after we've let them in."

Once again he picked up the handset for the outboard speakers. "Mandy, tell me what color bathing suit you wore on our date last Friday."

"Tom, what are you talking about?" Mandy demanded, shouting above the reply of the unmoving decoy. The gas mask muffled her words a bit, but the voice sounded real enough to Tom. "Nobody wears a bathing suit to the movies, even in California! Are you going to let us in, or not?"

"As soon as we're out of here," Tom promised. "PIPP says the room is full of poison gas. You and Sandra climb up onto TANC's hood and hang on until we get you someplace a bit safer."

The two girls clambered up onto TANC's oversize wheels and from there onto the hood. Then the huge vehicle used its trick of turning on its own length to change direction so that its nose pointed toward the light and air outside.

"Open the door, PIPP," Tom said as soon as TANC had gotten clear of the hidden bunker. "Let the girls in."

This time the right-hand side door of the cab lifted open. The girls slid down from the hood and climbed into the cab. TANC's wing-like door closed after them.

Peter Newell and Bill Kane moved farther back in the rear of TANC to let the two girls take their seats. "Welcome back," Newell said. "We were worried about you."

"We were worried about you, too," Sandra said, stripping off her gas mask as she spoke. "Mandy spotted those mannequins on the control room monitors. Bradshaw must have planted my locator on one of the mannequins to trap you, and as soon as I saw the gas masks on the wall, I figured out what the decoys were for. I was afraid you guys would be dumb enough to unseal the doors before we could get out there and warn you."

"You can thank PIPP that we didn't," said Tom. "TANC's sensors picked up on the gas, and PIPP wouldn't let us open up for the decoys."

"Good for him—it—whatever," said Sandra. "Now what are our plans?"

"Get airborne," said Tom, "and head for

home. We've got only a couple of little problems to work out first."

While this conversation was going on, TANC was cruising around the secret base. Heavy black smoke filled the sky, and little bands of Bradshaw's mercenaries kept popping out from behind rocks and buildings to fire small arms at the vehicle as it went by.

"We're getting a lot of radio traffic from the northeast," PIPP reported.

Peter Newell looked curious. "I thought you said this prototype didn't have communications."

"Ears only," said Tom. "They're part of TANC's basic sensor and testing setup. But no voice comms just yet. Those radio signals, PIPP. Can you read them?"

"No," PIPP replied. "They seem to be coded."

A split second later TANC veered suddenly, and a close explosion threw clods of dirt and stones against the side of the vehicle. Where TANC had been was now a smoking crater.

"What was that?" gasped Mandy.

"I can make a guess," said Rick. Tom's friend was looking at the monitor screen showing the landscape off to one side. "Bradshaw's an arms dealer, right?"

"Right," said Tom and Bill Kane together.

"And some of the arms he deals in are tanks and artillery, right?"

Kane nodded. "Right again."

"Well, here they come—mostly some things that look like extra-fancy armored cars. They have tank-type turrets, but they're on balloon wheels. And they're moving up on us fast."

"The signals must have been meant for them," said Tom. "Too bad we don't know what Bradshaw told them to do."

"I suspect," said Bill Kane as another explosion pockmarked the desert floor a few feet away, "that it was something on the order of Dead men tell no tales."

"You may be right," Tom conceded. "PIPP, can you pick it up some?"

"I don't think so," TANC's AI brain replied. "I'm already running at top speed for this terrain. I don't want to flip myself over."

"Anything that looks like a straight enough run for you to transform to a jet and take off?"

"Nothing. The terrain here is too broken."

"On the next prototype," Tom said, "I'll have to add vertical takeoff and landing capacity. Somebody remind me when we get back to the lab—Bradshaw's got my electronic notebook."

A shell burst directly in front of them. "Sorry," said PIPP. "Based on my analysis of the trajectories and energy levels of the projectiles, it'll be a while before we're out of range."

"Head for the landing strip," suggested Sandra. "Let's change to jet mode and get out of here."

"Uh, that's one of the 'little problems' we have to deal with," Rick said as another explosion rocked TANC and its passengers. "We destroyed the landing strip."

Mandy and Sandra looked at each other. "You destroyed the landing strip," said Sandra. "I should have known."

"Don't worry," Tom said. "PIPP, can you find us someplace flat enough to use for takeoff?"

"I'm sorry, Tom," PIPP replied. "I don't have digitized maps of this area."

Tom glanced over at Peter Newell. The NASA rep looked as if he didn't know whether he was horrified or fascinated. "When we go operational," Tom told him, "the full-size version of TANC will have digitized maps of the entire world. Furthermore, it will be able to construct its own maps of the moon, Mars, wherever it goes, from orbit, before touching down."

"That's not remarkably helpful now," Bill Kane put in. "What do we have on board that can help us now?"

"A GEOS satellite will come over soon," PIPP said. "I can read the information from it."

"Meanwhile, just keep us alive," Tom

ordered. "And, everybody, keep your eyes open."

TANC bumped over another series of rocky ridges and headed out into the Catamarca desert, a cloud of dust rising in its wake. Artillery shells still smashed all around, kicking up stones and dirt. Bradshaw's armored cars were in hot pursuit behind them. Up ahead the mountains grew nearer and nearer until they filled the entire horizon—the vast and impenetrable wall of the Andes.

"I think," Tom said, "that we're in serious trouble."

HIGHER AND HIGHER THE SNOWCAPPED mountains loomed ahead of Tom and his friends. The armored cars were drawing closer in their pursuit, and the crash of gunfire echoed constantly. TANC's outer armor and its agility kept its passengers safe—that, plus PIPP's capacity for predicting where a round would land before it hit.

"Excuse me," PIPP said. "I've just thought of something."

"Anything you've got, I want to hear," Tom replied. "What is it?"

"Well," PIPP replied, "you may recall that last week Sandra spent some time in programming me. Your sister was most thorough. In addition to the standard reference works and data bases, she also read into my memory the complete Swift family history."

"I don't see how Tom's ancestors are going to save our bacon right now," commented Rick.

"Be quiet, Rick," Tom said. "Let PIPP talk."

"I was doing random recombinations of data stored in memory," said PIPP, "in an attempt to find a way out of our current dilemma, when I chanced to superimpose the outline of these mountains upon a sketch from your grandfather's memoirs."

"You're saying that the mountain range reminded you of something you read?" Sandra asked eagerly.

"An organic intelligence might put it that way," said PIPP. "But in essence, yes. Your grandfather, in his youth, was involved in an engineering project to construct a tunnel through the Andes."

"The Andes cover a lot of area," Sandra said. "I remember those notes, too, and Grandfather never did say exactly where his tunnel was located. The project would have been a great thing for South America, he said, except that the highways and railroads that were supposed to feed into the tunnel never got built."

"I know that," PIPP said. "But after looking at the mountains around us and matching them against the description he gave, I believe we're in the right area."

"Even if we do find the tunnel," said Rick, "what good will it do us?"

"It'll let us get away from those guys," Sandra said. She pointed at her monitor screen, where a puff of smoke showed that one of the armored cars had just let loose another cannon shot. PIPP changed direction abruptly to avoid the round, throwing the TANC's passengers against their safety webbing.

"You won't get away as long as they're on top of you like that," Kane said. "If they see where you went, they'll follow."

Tom looked at the FBI agent. "Have you got a better idea?"

"Yes. We still have all the parts for a Tallis Cannon. I know how to assemble one, too. There should be just enough time for me to put together the firing mechanism, attach the power module, and get off a blast before Bradshaw's men enter the tunnel. Drop me off at the entrance to the tunnel, and I'll blow the back door shut once you're away."

"That's suicide," said Tom. "We can fire off the cannon from inside the tunnel—if we ever find it—and take you with us."

Kane shook his head. "You know better than that, Tom. Using the Tallis Cannon inside a confined space could bring the entire mountainside down on us. I'll have to set it up in the open and take my chances with Bradshaw later."

"Maybe not." To Tom's surprise, it was Peter Newell who spoke up. "We still have the Swift Enterprises portable helicopter I flew to the Arroyo Seco Autodrome. It's not much of a getaway vehicle, but it's better than slogging across the Catamarca on foot."

"Or waiting around for the bad guys to catch you," added Rick. "Take the chopper. If you crash it, Tom's dad can always send the FBI a bill for the parts."

Still Tom hesitated. Suppose Kane had really been working for Bradshaw all along, as a double agent to win Tom's trust in case threats didn't work? Bradshaw's mind worked that way—the Sandra and Mandy decoys were proof enough. What if Kane's brave offer was nothing more than a last-ditch attempt to get the parts for a Tallis Cannon?

I have to believe him, Tom decided. Because much as I hate to admit it, he's right about using a Tallis Cannon inside the tunnel.

"Okay," Tom said. "PIPP, find us that tunnel."

TANC had already slowed down and was now casting back and forth across the landscape like a hunting dog trying to pick up a trail.

"It should be right around here somewhere," PIPP said: "Some landmarks may have changed in the last eighty years or your grandfather's memory might have been a little off . . ."

TANC halted at the foot of a rocky escarpment. "It's here," PIPP announced. "I'm sure of it."

"That looks like solid rock to me," said Rick.

"I don't think so," PIPP replied. "The echoes are all wrong for that. Let's test it out."

Without warning, the vehicle sprang forward at the side of the cliff. But instead of unyielding stone, TANC's nose met only a thin layer of plaster and wood. The camouflage wall crumpled and fell away, and the tunnel mouth stood open in front of them.

"Here we are, Tom," said PIPP. "If Mr. Kane intends to block the entrance behind us, I suggest that he set up the cannon in the shelter of that big rock over to our right. It should provide him with protection from Bradshaw's artillery for a little while, at least."

Bill Kane straightened his shoulders. "All right, Tom. It looks as if we've got a couple of minutes' breathing space before the bad guys show up. Let's unload so you can get moving again."

"You heard him, PIPP," said Tom. "Open up."

TANC's door opened. Everybody on board swarmed out and began pushing out the boxes and crates that had been loaded into the cargo bay. Last of all, Tom handed over the portable helicopter to the FBI agent.

"I still don't believe that a working helicopter could weigh less than sixty pounds," Newell said, shaking his head. "And I flew the thing."

"Believe it," Rick advised him. "I've flown ultralights that didn't weigh much more than that, and you can buy those off the rack these days."

Tom was standing with Kane beside the folded rotary-wing aircraft. "Hit the blue switch to prepare the helicopter for operation," he told the FBI man. "Then stand back at least five feet until it's finished opening up. It's supposed to home in on a fixed destination, but there's a manual override for emergencies. You'll probably want to use that instead."

"I can manage," said Kane. He had already begun opening boxes and removing parts, counting them off under his breath as he worked. "Resonator, accelerator ... Don't just stand there, head on out while you have a chance."

"Right," said Tom. "And, Bill—good luck." He slammed shut the outer door of the cargo bay and climbed aboard TANC. The other passengers were already inside.

"Close the door, PIPP," he said. "It's time for us to go."

TANC rolled forward into the tunnel. The vehicle's headlights switched on, their brilliant beams slicing away the darkness that soon pressed in from all sides.

"Where does this tunnel come out?" Newell asked.

"The side of a mountain in Chile," said PIPP.

"Better pick up the speed as much as possible," Tom advised. "It's probably not a good idea for us to be inside when Kane shuts down the Catamarcan end."

"My sensors show a straight road in good condition," said PIPP. "I'll take it as fast as I can."

TANC's AI brain proved as good as its word. Going to emergency override mode, the vehicle's speed increased steadily until the velocity monitor read more than two hundred kilometers per hour. The walls of the tunnel streaked past in a shadowy blur. At one point the roadway entered a large subterranean chamber, where the shapes of what looked like buildings rose up in the darkness beyond the glare of the headlights.

"The Lost City of the Andes," said Sandra quietly. "Another reason why Granddad kept quiet about the location of the tunnel. The city was supposed to be preserved for archaeologists to study, and when the tunnel project didn't work out, he was afraid that looters would wreck the site."

"Well, they won't learn about it from us," said Tom. "Do you understand what I mean, PIPP?"

"I will purge the data from my memory banks as soon as we're safely away, Tom," the AI brain replied. "We don't have much farther to go."

"I hope not," Rick replied. "I'm starved. You guys got hot dogs yesterday, but I'm doing all this on an empty stomach."

Soon after, a reddish light showed at the end of the tunnel, as if they were riding directly into the setting sun. "Coming up on the end," PIPP announced. "What do you want me to do?"

"Stop for a moment," Tom ordered. "I'd like to see what's waiting for us before we stick our heads out."

"Understood," said PIPP. "Shall I extend a sensor unit?"

"Do that," said Tom. "Then show us the view on screen."

TANC halted a few feet away from the tunnel's mouth. A thin, flexible rod emerged from the vehicle's front and angled around the edge of the opening. One of the monitor

screens at the back of the cab blinked and
began displaying a new picture. TANC's passengers crowded around to look.

"Hoo-boy!" Rick exclaimed. "You were
talking about no roads or railways, but this
is worse. It looks like there isn't *anything* at
this end!"

He was right. Whatever open ground might
have waited in Tom's grandfather's day for
the coming of mountain highways and nar-
row-gauge railroads waited there no longer.
At some time since then, a landslide or ava-
lanche had tumbled down the side of the
mountain, turning the slope below the tunnel's mouth into a packed mass of jagged
rock.

"Shall I go on?" asked PIPP.

Tom hesitated for a moment. It was hard
to judge size from the picture on the monitor
screen, but the boulders looked as big as
houses.

But before anyone could answer PIPP's
question, a sound like distant thunder filled
the tunnel—a deep, sustained vibration that
set various bits and pieces of gear inside
TANC humming in sympathy.

"The Tallis Cannon," breathed Mandy when
the shaking had ended. "It must have collapsed the entire other end of the tunnel. We
can't go back now even if we want to."

16

IF WE CAN'T GO BACK, WE HAVE TO GO FORWARD," said Tom. "PIPP, can you transform here in the tunnel and take off as if this were a landing strip?"

"I can," PIPP replied.

"Good," said Tom with relief. "You won't be able to extend the wings, but if you get going fast enough you'll have time to get them out before we hit. It'll be just like on the proving ground."

"Good enough," Rick said. "Let's do it."

TANC backed up well into the tunnel and began its limited transformation. Within seconds the ground vehicle was a wingless aircraft.

"Here we go," said PIPP.

Rick laughed. "If this works, just call us the Silicon Condor."

TANC had taken the underground road at high speed, but its speed now, as PIPP sought to gain velocity for takeoff, was even higher. The mouth of the tunnel drew rapidly closer. The red glare of sunset splashed across the vehicle's windshield, the ground dropped away beneath them, and they were out.

The passengers knew an instant of stomach-twisting free-fall. Then PIPP unfolded TANC's wings, fired up the nuclear-powered turbines, and they were away.

"Take us north," Tom said. "Back to Swift Enterprises."

Sandra looked at the radar screen. "We've got trouble," she said. "Surface-to-air missiles, heading straight at us!"

"I was afraid of that," Tom said. "Bradshaw must have figured out where we would come out of the tunnel."

The missiles came closer, plumes of white smoke trailing behind them.

"Impact in twenty seconds," PIPP said. "They're locked on and tracking."

"And I know *what* they're tracking!" Tom exclaimed. As he spoke, he stripped off his belt, with the buckle containing the personnel locator. He tossed the belt into a small compartment labeled Sample Ejection Port and pressed the Cycle button.

A couple of seconds later a brilliant flash lit up the TANC's monitors.

"One of the missiles got your belt buckle," said Sandra. "But the others must be heat seekers. They're still following us." Tom saw her swallow hard. "Impact in five seconds."

Abruptly the jet pointed its nose at the zenith and accelerated. "I didn't have time to ask permission," PIPP said, its synthesized voice unaffected by a maneuver that had the human passengers pressed hard against the cushions of their seats. "But I judge that outrunning the missiles is our best bet."

"How are we doing on that?" Tom asked after he'd caught his breath.

"Holding even," Sandra reported from her place by the status board. "The missiles aren't gaining, but they aren't losing, either."

"You don't suppose it's the Chilean Air Force that shot at us?" Peter Newell asked. "We did enter their airspace without permission, after all."

"No," PIPP said. "I don't think so. Those missiles are SA-fifty-sevens. According to the references I've read, Chile doesn't have any of those."

"But Arthur Bradshaw obviously does," Sandra said. "And they're still coming. Tom, what are we going to do?"

"I think I know what comes next," her

brother replied. "We can let PIPP handle things for a while."

The jet-form TANC rose higher and higher. The altimeter on its control panel scrolled to the right as the sun came out from behind the curve of the earth, rising in the west like a backward dawn. But in spite of the returning sun the sky outside the windshield darkened steadily, going from deep blue to an even deeper black. A few stars came out.

"Losing air to the jets, losing lift," PIPP announced. "Changing modes, now!"

Again the outside of TANC transformed: The wings folded in, solar heat-exchangers folded out, and the jets retracted into the body. Fusion-powered rocket engines deployed at the rear, and a vibration throughout the craft told Tom that the engines were firing. New signal lights blinked on across the control panel to relay the same information.

"Surface-to-air missiles dropping away," Sandra announced. "Looks like we won this round."

"The credit for that should go to PIPP," said Tom. "We've just gone orbital."

Peter Newell gazed about with something like awe on his bony features. "Ever since I was a kid," he murmured, half to himself, "I've dreamed of going into space. That's why I joined NASA. But I couldn't get into the astronaut program. I thought that seeing the pictures was the closest I'd ever come. But now ... this is wonderful."

"Not quite *that* wonderful," Tom said. "This mode wasn't set for testing for another three weeks. We don't have any of the re-breathers installed and charged, or the oxygen recycling mechanisms. Which means that the air we have is all the air we're going to get."

"How long does that give us?" Newell asked.

"Maybe half an hour," said Tom. "PIPP, if anything goes wrong, get us back to Swift Enterprises. Meanwhile, since we're up here, let's take the shortest way home."

"Do you want the shortest way or the quickest?" PIPP asked. "The quickest is once around the globe and in, dropping back into the atmosphere right over California. The shortest is a straight line from here to there, but that way would take us a little longer."

"Quickest, then," Rick said. "I could use a double pizza with everything on it, and I don't want to wait a minute more than I have to."

Tom laughed. "Quickest," he agreed.

TANC, in its spacegoing form, sailed on over the south Atlantic Ocean, spiraling up across Africa and the Indian Ocean toward the eastern Pacific and home. The sun glinted off the planet below them—the swirls of white cloud, the dusty browns and deep greens of the land, and the sparkling blue of the water.

"Look at the sunset line," Tom said after several minutes had passed. "It'll be night when we get back."

"You told Dad you'd be home after dark," Sandra pointed out. "You just didn't tell him which day."

"Coming up on deceleration for reentry," PIPP said.

"Take us in over the ocean outside of U.S. territorial waters," Tom said. "We don't need to have U.S. Space Command or Air Defenses get nervous about us."

"Okay," PIPP replied. "Stand by—now!"

Using the lateral jets, PIPP rotated TANC until it was falling around the earth tail-first. Then the spacecraft's main engines fired, reducing TANC's speed down to below orbital levels. The altimeter began scrolling to the left.

"Hold on," Tom called. "Going down!"

TANC's carbonite heatshield guarded them as they descended, while the glow of ionized air surrounded them. And then they were into the lower atmosphere.

"Okay, PIPP," Tom said. "Convert back to jet mode, and let's head for home."

There was a pause. "I have a problem," PIPP said.

Tom's stomach sank. "What kind of problem?"

"TANC won't convert. I've run the routine twice now."

"Try it again—fast!"

"I am already trying a third time," said PIPP. "It's no good. We have three minutes until impact."

None of TANC's passengers said anything. Tom knew they were all probably too scared to speak. Falling from this height into the Pacific Ocean, hitting the water would be like hitting concrete.

Nobody on board would survive.

17

Tom forced himself to speak calmly. "Is this a mechanical problem, PIPP, or a programming bug?"

"I can't tell," the machine answered.

Tom unstrapped himself. He bumped around the cabin in free-fall and began pulling himself hand-over-hand to the deck at the rear of the cabin, beside Sandra's control panel.

"Tool kit!" he called to his sister. "Quick!"

Sandra looked as pale as skim milk, and her eyes were wide with fear. Her hands were steady, though, as she unhooked a roll of tools from the bulkhead and handed them to Tom. Moving as fast as he dared—he couldn't risk fumbling something and then having to waste precious seconds retrieving it—he unscrewed a deckplate and peered inside.

"Not good," he said. "The conversion routine is loaded from outside of TANC's cab."

"Two minutes till splashdown," Sandra said. Her voice shook a little. "And I do mean splash."

"Okay," Tom said. "I'm going to go manual on this."

He jerked a wrench out of the tool kit and threw it down into the tangle of wires below him.

"What on earth are you doing?" exclaimed Newell.

"Trying to disconnect the computer yoke the hard way," Tom replied without looking around. He threw another wrench. The ends of the bundle of wires he'd been aiming at floated free. "Aha! That did it!"

He pulled out his smart shoelace. Oblivious to Peter Newell's spluttered questions, he straightened the lace between his fingers. It stayed straight. With his body pressed against the deckplates and his arm as deep inside the access hole as he could get it, the tip of the shoelace just reached the bundle of wires.

"One minute," Sandra said.

Tom tweaked the end of his shoelace. It tied itself around the bundle of wires in a neat bowknot. He pulled the wires up toward him.

"Let's see, now. I *think* that I need to short the blue wire to the yellow wire."

Peter Newell made a kind of gobbling sound. "What if you're wrong?"

"Thirty seconds," said Sandra.

"Then I'll try something different," said Tom. He twisted the ends of the two wires together.

The nose of TANC elongated to the jet-mode's glittering needle, and the wings deployed. Everyone heaved a sigh of relief.

"All right," Tom said. Then lift took over, TANC abruptly slowed, and Tom was thrown against the front wall of the cabin. "Oof!" he exclaimed.

"Are you okay, Tom?" Mandy cried out.

"A couple of bruises, nothing bad," he said, rubbing his arms and legs. "How are we doing, PIPP?"

"Normal flight attitude," PIPP replied. "We were over maximum acceleration, but the wings didn't fall off when they opened. You build good gear, Tom."

"You did pretty well for yourself, PIPP," Tom said. "I'm proud of you."

"Thank you, Tom," said the AI brain. "I'm glad to know that I didn't let down the Swift tradition. I hope you don't mind—since you constructed me and Sandra programmed me, I can't help thinking of myself as being at least a distant relative."

Sandra laughed. "I can't speak for everybody, PIPP, but you can call me 'cousin' any time you want."

"Thank you, Cousin Sandra," said PIPP formally. "We're coming up now on the coast of California, near Central Hills. This area is in my digital maps. Shall I convert to terrestrial mode and return to Swift Enterprises by highway?"

"Sounds good to me," said Tom. "Fewer headaches for the air traffic controllers, especially since we don't have communications."

"Terrestrial mode it is, then," said PIPP. TANC went into a steep dive, pulled out at the last minute above Route 34, and extended its wheels. Soon the vehicle was taxiing through the night along the deserted highway, wings still extended.

"You may have to check the emergency rewiring job," said PIPP. "I'm having trouble transforming again."

"No problem." The young inventor went to the back and picked up the bundle of wires. "Here goes."

But nothing Tom did to the wires would let PIPP complete the transformation. He looked down through the access plate and shook his head. "Appears that one of those wrenches I threw got tangled in the mechanism for withdrawing the wing surfaces. We're going to be a little wide."

"Wow," said Rick. "A monster truck with wings."

"It's okay," said Tom. "We're almost home. We'll be at Swift Enterprises before long."

"Or maybe not," said Mandy. "Look— there's a police roadblock up ahead. We're going to have to pull over."

It was true. The glare of TANC's headlights showed two police cars blocking the highway, parked nose to nose across the lanes. A line of safety flares ahead of them warned of their presence, and a row of stopped cars bordered the road on either side.

"Something must have happened in town while we were gone," said Rick. "A bank robbery, maybe, or a jailbreak. And we probably look pretty suspicious."

"Everything will be okay once they talk to Dad," Sandra reassured him. "He'll get it straightened out."

"I don't know," said Tom slowly as he looked out the front window at the roadblock. Even from this distance he could see that one of the police officers at the checkpoint had one arm in a sling.

That doesn't seem right, he thought. The police wouldn't need to put someone with an injury out in front.

"PIPP," he said, "give me a magnified image of those police officers."

"Already magnifying," said PIPP. "Check the number-two monitor."

Tom looked at the screen. In the close-up picture the injured cop had a very familiar face. He was O'Malley's buddy from the auto-drome, the fake FBI agent whose arm Tom had injured in his brief struggle to escape.

"It's a setup!" Tom exclaimed. "Don't stop, PIPP. Break through and keep right on moving. Just try not to hurt any bystanders while you're doing it."

"No civilian casualties," PIPP replied. "Do you have any philosophical objections to property damage?"

"Nope. We're insured."

"Then hold on!"

TANC accelerated suddenly and kept on going, the still-extended wings providing lift. With a heavy thump TANC's wheels hit the roof of one police car, bouncing them into the air. "Without the practice at Arroyo Seco I never would have had the knowledge to try that," PIPP said as they touched the road beyond the farthest car.

A few miles farther on, a chain-link fence and gate stretched across the road. "The back of the proving grounds," said Tom. "Keep on going, PIPP. We can't open the gate, so we might as well knock it down."

They broke through into the proving grounds. On they ran, moving at high speed over the course they had followed the morning before, smashing past the guard post into the main Swift Enterprises complex and coming at last to a halt before the robotic hangar, where TANC had been built.

"Everybody out," Tom said. "PIPP, open the doors."

The doors lifted, and everyone tumbled to the ground. "I feel like kissing the pavement," Newell said, but the NASA rep was smiling as he spoke. "On the other hand, I just had the ride of my life. I never expected to see such high performance under stress from a prototype model. If this is what you Swifts can do with a first-generation vehicle, I think I can recommend both PIPP and TANC without reservation to my superiors back in Washington."

All at once a bright light glared out of the night, and an amplified voice said, "Okay, hands up. Real slow."

"Harlan Ames, is that you?" Tom called.

"Tom?" The security chief strode out of the darkness, a relieved expression on his face. "You aren't wearing your locator. We've been at a Class One alert ever since you disappeared from Arroyo Seco. Let's get over to your dad's office and let him know you're home."

As they walked, Tom explained to Harlan Ames about the fake police roadblock. Ames listened intently and then put a call through to the Central Hills Police Department from his pocket phone. What he heard made him chuckle.

"The police are bringing those guys in right now," he reported to Tom after the conversation had ended. "When you and TANC smashed through the roadblock the way you did, a civilian driver who'd already been stopped called the cops on his cellular phone to report your escape. Which surprised the CHPD all to pieces, because they hadn't put up any roadblocks to catch anybody. After that it didn't take Chief Montague long to put two and two together and send over a couple of *real* squad cars."

"So much for the local end of Arthur Bradshaw's operation," said Mandy. "But I hate to think of that man sitting down there in Argentina out of reach."

"I don't like it, either," said Tom. "But I suppose you take what you can get."

When the group reached the office of Thomas Swift, Tom's father was hanging up the telephone. His worried expression vanished as soon as Tom and the others walked through the door.

"Thank goodness you're all safe," he said, enveloping his son and daughter in a warm hug. "I just got off the phone with Bill Kane in Buenos Aires. He said the last he'd seen of you was somewhere down in the Andes."

"Kane's safe?" Tom asked. "That's great! When he insisted on staying behind to close off our getaway route, I didn't know if we'd ever see him again."

"He's fine," said Tom's father. "After he blew up the tunnel entrance, he destroyed the Tallis Cannon and escaped just as Bradshaw's mercenaries were closing in. The portable helicopter got shot up a bit while he was making his getaway, but it held together long enough for Kane to reach an Argentine police barracks and tell his story."

Mr. Swift smiled. "It seems that the legitimate government hadn't realized exactly what was going on up in that desolate corner of the Catamarca. Bradshaw had told them it was a mining project, and they weren't happy to find out they'd been lied to all along. The Argentine military is moving in to shut down the entire operation, and our ambassador to Argentina thinks we've got a good chance at getting Bradshaw extradited for trial."

"That ties up the loose ends, all right," said Tom.

"Not quite," Rick said. "We still have one problem."

Tom looked curiously at his friend. "What's that?"

"Dinner," said Rick. "I don't know about

you, but I haven't eaten since this adventure started, and I'm hungry!"

Tom laughed. "Don't worry. As soon as Sandra and I let Mom know we're okay, we can all go out for pizza. TANC is out of commission for a while, but we can take the van—" Tom stopped when he saw the looks on everyone's faces. "Or," he added with a grin, "we can call for a delivery."

Tom's next adventure:

Tom and his pals are in the south Atlantic, soaking up the sun and testing his ultra high-tech diving gear, including a powerful underwater laser beam and minisub. But the ocean abyss is a strange and sinister place, and Tom is working in dangerous waters—smack in the middle of the infamous Bermuda Triangle!

After several cargo ships vanish without a trace, Tom spots what appears to be an enormous sea monster flanked by a troop of armed underwater commandos. The discovery leads him to a confrontation with a ruthless nemesis from his past—a criminal genius who has hatched an explosive scheme to spread terror from beneath the sea . . . in Tom Swift #6, *Aquatech Warriors*.